A Sugarplum Wish

More by Kari Shuey

WISHING FOR LOVE SERIES

A Gingerbread Wish

A Candycane Wish

A Sugarplum Wish

A Cranberry Wish - Coming Dec 2025

A Peppermint Wish - Coming Dec 2026

More to be announced...

SECURITECH INC SERIES

The Last Housekeeper

Her Deadly Defender

The Phantom Code

HEART HEIST SERIES

Securing the Sapphire

Ransoming the Rubies

Protecting the Pearls

SWEET ROMANCE STANDALONES

That Crazy Girl Upstairs

Solitaire's Lucky Match

MATHIAS SERIES WITH ANGELA PERRY

Boston 2009

Mathias: Cutthroat

Mathias: Vice Versa

Mathias: Night Shift

Mathias: Light Keeper (coming soon)

A Sugarplum Wish

WISHING FOR LOVE

CHRISTMAS IN BRECKENRIDGE
BOOK TWO

KARI SHUEY

Copyright © 2024 by Kari Shuey

All rights reserved.

No part of this book may be reproduced in any form or by any electronic or mechanical means, including information storage and retrieval systems, without written permission from the author, except for the use of brief quotations in a book review.

Chapter 1

SCARLETT

"What do you mean it's *gone*?" I snap, digging a hand into my blonde hair with growing anxiety.

"I'm sorry, Miss Winters. I've checked your name three times—"

"I've had an account with you for over five years. You can't tell me all my money just disappeared. There was at least eighty thousand dollars in that account a few months ago." I can't keep my voice from shaking. This can't be happening. Everything was going so well. There's no way this is happening. Not now. Not when everything I want is finally within reach. I lurch in my pacing, coming to a stop in front of my kitchen table. The apartment over the ice-skating rink was a bonus—and something that sealed the deal two years ago. I swallow hard, picking up the notice from the bank with shaking hands. I can't believe I'm only now seeing this. "I want to speak to Kevin."

"I'm sorry?" the timid voice on the other end asks softly. "Kevin?"

I close my eyes tight and take a deep breath, though it doesn't help like I want it to. "Mr. Murphy. I need to speak to my financial advisor." He's been my manager since I competed in the winter Olympics a few years ago. I pinch the bridge of my nose, realizing it has been a hot minute since I heard from him.

There is an odd sort of silence that hangs in the air between me and the poor girl on the other end of the line. She's new. I can almost guarantee it.

Heaving another sigh, I lean against the table, putting my full body weight on my left hand. "Just... please... connect me with—"

"I'm sorry. I'll get my manager."

"Thank you," I murmur. There has to be a reasonable explanation for all of this. Everything will right itself the minute I speak to someone who has authority. The hand holding the phone to my ear trembles slightly. All that money. If it is gone, I don't know what I'll do. There's no way I can afford to pay for the Ice Castle rink from the money I'm bringing in. Most businesses don't make a profit in the first couple of years. According to my records, the amount I'm bringing in is going up. I just need the cushion I built up in my account.

"Hello? Miss Winters?"

I breathe a sigh of relief. "Yes, thank you for speaking with me—"

"I'm so sorry to tell you this..." the man on the other end starts.

My arm buckles beneath my weight as his words penetrate my

soul. I collapse on the kitchen chair. Words like authorities, theft, and untraceable knock the wind right from my lungs.

"We're so sorry you were not contacted. We're still trying to find all the accounts that were affected."

"Gone?" I whisper with a raspy voice. "All of it? Don't you have insurance? Isn't there something we can do?"

"Unfortunately, there are several factors concerning this issue. We're going to do our best..." The man's voice fades, replaced by the thrashing sound of blood rushing in my ears. I'm dizzy. What am I going to do? I don't have much in my checking account—just enough to put food on the table.

The ice-skating rink is my whole world. I can't lose it.

My breaths come out in sharp, short breaths. I may actually pass out right here, right now.

Placing my arm on the table, I gently rest my face into its crook. I can barely speak as I mumble, "Yes, please send me the information I need to file a report."

My phone falls to the table with a clatter. I don't know what I'm going to do. The past due letter on the table indicates I haven't made the last three payments. It's my fault, really. I trusted the account was in good standing. And I'm terrible at opening all my mail.

Memories of a childhood wrought with poverty fill my mind. Helpless. Hopeless. That little girl had always had to depend on everyone else for everything. I'd clawed my way out of that life. I'd sworn to myself I'd never go back.

But look at me now?

A tear streaks down my cheek, cool liquid slicing across my hot skin. I don't have anywhere to go. There's no way I'll qualify for a loan that can help me through this slump—not that I want to go deeper into debt than the mortgage and business loans I already have.

I lose track of time. I may have even fallen asleep—there's no way to tell. My phone buzzes on the table, startling me. Slowly, I lift my head and watch the small rectangular object skitter across the table with each vibration.

Briefly, I consider not answering. Holly will understand. She knows I could be busy. Without really thinking what the consequences will be, I grab the phone and put it to my ear. "Hello?" I crack.

"Hey!" A pause. "Scarlett?" This time Holly's voice is more tentative, more concerned. "What's wrong?" she demands. "I'm coming over."

That escalated quickly.

I heave a shuddering sigh and wipe at my hot, swollen eyes. "No. Don't come. Can we meet in town? I could use some chocolate."

Silence. It weighs on me much like the silence from the supervisor. Then, "Sure. Stella's?"

My eyes sweep through my small apartment. At this point, it may be a bad idea to go out. I don't exactly have the budget to go out—not even to get one piece of chocolate at Stella's. I swallow the lump in my throat. "Actually, maybe you should come over."

Holly has got to be the most intuitive person in my life. I don't know how she does it, but she has the ability to make me feel seen and heard all at once. "Nope. You're coming out with me. Stella's. Twenty minutes. My treat."

I want to sob right then and there. I want to tell her everything over the phone because if I have to tell her in person, I know I'll be a blubbering mess. But Holly doesn't give me a chance to do so.

"Twenty minutes," she repeats. "Out front. If you don't show, I'm getting Lucian's truck and I'm dragging your sorry self out of that rink."

A ghost of a smile touches my lips, and I nod, even though I know she can't see me. Holly hangs up before I do. For the next ten minutes, I do my best to clean off my smudged makeup and reapply some to hide that I've been crying. Then I grab my coat and head out the door.

THE REFROZEN SNOW CRUNCHES BENEATH OUR BOOTS as Holly and I wander down the main sidewalk in town toward our favorite sweet spot. Eva is arguably one of the best bakers on the continent. No one will be able to convince me otherwise. She can make any treat into something divine.

"So... what's going on?" Holly asks quietly.

I shrug.

"Don't give me that. I heard it in your voice. Something is up." She reaches for my arm and pulls me around to look me full in the face. "You have to tell me. That's what friends do."

She's one of the few people in my life I consider a friend and probably the only one who can understand what I'm going through. I take a deep breath and then release it. "Kevin—my financial manager—he lost all of my money." I scrunch up my forehead. "Or he stole it. This whole thing is a little foggy."

Holly gasps, a hand flying to her mouth. "*What?*"

"Yeah. It really sucks because he did it a few months ago, and now I'm behind on my payments for the rink." I don't think it's possible, but Holly's eyes grow wider.

"You're kidding," she breathes. Then she blinks several times and shakes her head. "What about insurance? What is the company doing for you?"

My face flushes so deep I feel like I walked right into a pizza oven. I can't meet her gaze as I mumble, "Because he brought my account over from when he was managing my career, it wasn't really brought into the umbrella of the company. I was grandfathered in some strange way." I shake my head, and tears sting my eyes. "I guess he was doing a lot of illegal things. They don't know what—if any—of my situation will be covered." I bite back a sob. I can't cry here on the side of the street. Someone might see.

"How much do you need? To get you clear with your bank, I mean?"

I cut her a look. "No, Holly."

"What? I can't offer to help?"

I shake my head. "I'm not asking for a handout."

"I know. I'm *offering.*" Holly places her hands on my shoulders, her bright, concerned eyes delving into mine as if she can see to the depths of my soul. "Let me help... just until you get on your feet."

Her words make my stomach churn. I hate that I even need help. I'm not going to let someone step in and rescue me. I was raised to understand that no one and nothing would come charging in on a white horse when times get tough. If I wanted to make something of myself, I had to do it on my own. I wanted to be a star skater, so I practiced until my feet bled. I clawed my way to the top. And then I tore my ACL, and everything crumbled after that.

I shake my head sharply. "I can't let you do that, and you know why."

"Because you're stubborn," she mutters.

"No," I drag out. "Because my rink is my dream. It's the one thing I wanted after my accident. I have to do it on my own." I will do it on my own—like I did before. I just don't know how, yet.

Holly rolls her eyes. "That doesn't mean you have to be alone in this. There's a reason we're drawn to making certain friends."

I force a smile. "You're too sweet for your own good."

"No, I just sorta like you."

Someone bumps into my right shoulder, and both Holly and I startle. He's a tall man dressed in a three-piece suit. His black shoes glint despite the overcast sky. A small girl is holding his hand. He glances over his shoulder to look my way before mumbling, "Apologies."

My eyes follow him, locking on the back of his head. I don't recognize his accent. It almost sounds like English and another language blended to make something new.

An elbow digs sharply into my side, and I jump again to find Holly grinning at me. Her brows bounce playfully. "Maybe you need something... else... to get your mind off this whole debacle."

I shove her shoulder. "That is something I definitely don't need. Right now, I have to focus on figuring out how to keep my rink."

"How long do you have?" Holly's expression is thoughtful again. "Please tell me they're going to be flexible with you."

"The day after Christmas," I sigh.

"That's in a few weeks!" Holly gasps. "Seriously? Scarlett, you have to let Lucian and me help you!"

I level a sharp look at her. "Don't make me tell you no again. I'm going to figure it all out. I just have to wrap my head around a few things, first."

Holly presses her lips together in a tight, thin line. It's clear by the look on her face that she doesn't feel comfortable with my statement. She's one of the best friends I have, and I don't know what I would do without her.

I pull her in for a hug, squeezing her tight. "Thank you," I whisper.

She steps back first and gives me a pointed stare. "Just remember that Lucian and I are here for you. No matter what—and especially if you change your mind."

I nod and brush at the tear that escapes down my cheek. "I know," I say hoarsely.

"Good. Now, let's get over to Stella's before Eva sells out of her homemade candy canes. They're to die for."

Chapter 2

KASPER

Annabelle tugs on my hand. "Dad, come *on*. You're too slow."

I drag my gaze from the two blonde women we just passed and glance down at my daughter with a smirk. "Maybe you're walking too fast. Ever think of that?" She's always been the kind of kid who can't sit still. I've tried everything from sports to dance and, so far, nothing is sticking.

She pulls on me some more. "I saw it. It's over here."

"What is?" I chuckle.

"The toy store," she groans. "I saw it yesterday."

"You can't possibly remember what you saw yesterday. We only *got here* yesterday—only drove down this street once." She's far too smart for her own good. I like to think she gets it from me, but if I'm honest with myself, I know that trait comes from her mother.

A twinge of sadness blossoms in my chest at the memory of

my late wife. Rose should be here with us, walking down the picturesque Idaho streets while holding onto our daughter's hand. She was stolen from my life too soon, leaving Annabelle without a mother.

"See? See? There it is!" Annabelle jumps up and down and points across the street. "They have a train in the window."

If I wasn't looking at the store with my own eyes, I would have never believed it. I stare down with surprise at my daughter who will be five in a few months. How on earth she remembers seeing this store is beyond my understanding.

A proud smile splits her face. Together, we walk to the end of the street so we can utilize the crosswalk. Perhaps if we can find a couple puzzles or some books, it will be enough to keep her busy while we stay at the local bed and breakfast. If I can avoid alienating the other guests due to Annabelle's high energy levels, I'll be happy.

The bell above the glass door jingles as we enter. A woman behind the counter offers a warm smile, and I nod in return.

"Wow," Annabelle whispers. "This place is so cool."

Overhead, toy planes hang suspended from the ceiling. The train visible from the window wraps around the perimeter of the store on a high shelf. Rows and rows of merchandise stand behind several displays of popular toys. It looks like we've just walked into Santa's workshop.

I glance down at my daughter, a broad smile on my face. "It's *totally* cool."

Her eyes sparkle with excitement, and she darts off, leaving me to follow. I shake my head with another chuckle. Annabelle is too brave for her own good. It's probably the armed security we usually have around us, though for the next few weeks they'll be absent. My parents, the current king and queen of Averna, aren't thrilled about my decision. But thankfully they're willing to listen to me. Their decision definitely has something to do with my needing space.

What safer place to find my center than a small town in the middle of nowhere?

I shove my hands in my pockets and stroll in my daughter's wake. Her attention bounces from shelf to shelf. Her excited chatter is almost enough to help me forget my reasons for coming to Breckenridge in the first place.

An escape.

We need an escape where people don't know who we are. So far, so good.

"Dad! Can I get this?" Annabelle jumps up and down holding a box that's half her size. It slips in her hands despite her white-tipped fingers.

I let out a low whistle. "I'm sorry, bug, but somehow I don't think Meredith will be thrilled with that choice."

She frowns, and my heart lurches like it always does when she turns those big brown eyes on me.

I drop down in front of her and gently remove the box from her clutches. "Slime and hotels don't mix."

Her lower lip protrudes, but she doesn't argue.

Placing the box on the shelf, I let my gaze sweep across the other crafts available in this section. "You could get this one." I pluck a smaller box from the shelf, knowing I'm going to regret it the second she breaks it open. "See? Friendship bracelets with glittery beads and rainbow string."

She eyes the box like I'm handing her a rodent.

"I'm certain Meredith would love it if you made her a friendship bracelet."

Annabelle brightens. The head housekeeper at The Gingerbread Cottage has taken a shining to the little girl at my feet. But it makes sense. Annabelle has a knack for wrapping everyone around her little finger, myself included. She snatches the box from my hands and hugs it to her chest. "Okay. Can I make one for you, too?"

"I'd be honored if you'd make me one."

Her smile returns, and I rise to my feet once more.

Holding out my hand, I jerk my chin toward an aisle that is clearly sporting puzzles of all shapes, sizes, and styles. "What do you say about getting a puzzle?"

Annabelle's face scrunches into what she probably thinks is disdain, but it only makes her look more adorable. Sheesh, I'm a sucker for this kid. She shakes her head. "Can we get paints instead?"

I grimace. Another messy activity. "How about a coloring book and crayons?"

She nods.

Never in my wildest dreams did I think I'd be negotiating with a child half my size. I suppose even princes of sovereign nations have to do things they aren't prepared for when it comes to their children.

We track down the art supplies, then make our way to the front of the store. The plump older woman rings up our purchases, and we're on our way once again.

Outside, there's no sign of the women I bumped into. It

wouldn't have made sense to see them with how long we were in the store. Something inside me yearns to get another look—like a tether linked me with them for some reason.

No, not both of them.

Just the one.

They were both blonde, but the one my shoulder had connected with had the most beautiful blue eyes I've ever seen, eyes that fairytales are made of. The town is small. Maybe I'll see her again.

I remind myself that I'm not here to meet anyone. My eyes dip down to where Annabelle skips at my side. I'm here to get my footing—as a father and the second in line for the crown.

I smile when Annabelle looks up at me as if sensing my attention. She smiles back and reaches for my hand.

THE GINGERBREAD COTTAGE IS BUSIER THAN I expected when I made my reservation a few months ago. People are constantly coming and going. More than once, I nearly bump into another guest.

After getting Annabelle set up with her coloring book, I wander down to the main sitting area. The first person I see is one of the blondes from earlier. She's not the one I bumped into, though, and I fight the disappointment that slithers through me. Dragging my eyes from where she sits at a booth within a bay window, I turn my focus to Meredith, who stands behind the reception desk.

I intend to ask Meredith for suggestions regarding activities in town, so I surprise myself when I lean forward and whisper, "Who's that?"

Meredith follows my gaze, and a knowing smile graces her lips. "She's familiar, huh?"

I can't bring myself to answer. That isn't why I'm asking. I'm curious if the other blonde will come up. If they were together earlier today, then they'll be together again. It's an assumption I'm willing to bet on.

The housekeeper leans forward and lowers her voice. "That's Holly. She's an author."

My brows lift. "She's a local?" I can't keep the surprise from my voice. What reason would she have for being at a bed and breakfast?

"She is now." Meredith's chuckle is low, and I feel warmth creep beneath my skin. "She's married, dear. If that's what you're wondering."

The heat intensifies, and I let loose an embarrassed laugh. "No, no. That's not—" I swallow hard and turn from Holly. "I bumped into her earlier. I didn't expect to see her in a place like this."

Meredith arches an amused brow.

Dang it. I'm normally so sure with my words, and I find myself stumbling for no plausible reason. "What I mean is… locals don't usually stay at a bed and breakfast, do they?"

Her smile widens, and she tilts her head as she watches me. "Her husband is the owner of this establishment."

Not even the sudden understanding I have in my grasp is enough to wash away the buffoonery I just put on full display. I nod and clear my throat, realizing I've forgotten my reasons for coming downstairs from my room. My eyes catch on a bright neon-green flyer. It's pinned to a bulletin board near the front desk.

Ice-skating Lessons for Children

The words draw me in. I've never thought about putting Annabelle in anything extracurricular besides what's common back home. She's taken riding lessons, violin lessons, and lessons in several languages. But ice-skating? It would help limit her screen time while on vacation.

"Your little girl would absolutely love working with Scarlett. She's amazing with children." Meredith's voice breaks into my thoughts, and I shift my focus to her. "She's the owner of the rink," Meredith continues, nodding to the flyer. "If you plan on staying for the whole month, I'd suggest reaching out to her."

My eyes drift to the flyer. I feel a strange sort of tug to it—as if it's trying to tell me something important. I move closer to the flyer and touch the corner with my finger. The office hours are wide open. And the rates for the group lessons are more than reasonable.

Except I'm not sure I want Annabelle in just group lessons. She does very well in one-on-one sessions with her tutors. I mull over the possibility of requesting both. What better way to get both our minds off everything we've endured in the last year than to spend time at a rink learning a new skill?

I nod to Meredith with a smile. "Thank you. I think we will. Is the rink far from here? Do I need to call a cab?"

Meredith shakes her head. "Around here, everything is within a reasonable walking distance." Her eyes brighten.

"Except the Frosted Wonderland. You'd need to catch a ride out there."

"Frosted Wonderland?" A vision of a castle carved from ice fills my mind—the structure similar to one of my daughter's favorite movies. "Is it something Annabelle would like to visit?"

"Most definitely. But they only open at night. There are lights and a sleigh ride and—" She slices a hand through the air. "You'll have to see for yourself. It's a little gem in this part of the state. You won't want to miss out."

Once again, I nod my gratitude just as the pitter-patter of feet scurry down the stairs. "Dad! I finished. What can we do now?"

Meredith grins at me as if to say I may as well head to the rink now.

I heave a sigh and reach out my hand toward Annabelle. I don't miss the look of curiosity I receive from the owner's wife, but she quickly looks back to her computer screen. Crouching in front of my daughter, I tuck her blonde hair behind her ear. "I was thinking I might sign you up for ice-skating lessons."

Annabelle's eyes round like saucers. "Really?"

"Really," I chuckle, rising and offering her my hand. "Let's go get your coat."

SCARLETT

"First group lesson will be tomorrow at four," I tell the mother on the other end of the phone. "I've got three other children signed up. Christopher will be able to make a few new friends."

"Oh, wonderful. Thank you so much, Scarlett."

"My pleasure." I hang up the phone and place it next to my small but growing roster. The flyers were only hung a couple hours ago. Holly insisted we get some printed and hung up immediately to help with my financial situation.

Part of me hates that I told her about it in the first place. I heave a sigh and fiddle the pencil between my finger and thumb. A whoosh of cold air rustles the papers before me.

"Welcome." I call out of habit. Then I lift my head, and my heart freezes. What are the chances that the man I bumped into—the man Holly teased could become a distraction—is walking right toward me? He's got warm brown hair and matching chestnut eyes. He's clean shaven, which is different than most of the men who live in Breckenridge. And he's wearing a suit. A suit! Who is this guy?

My eyes dip to the small girl clinging to his hand. She's adorable. Her blonde wispy hair falls around her shoulders in soft waves. Her brown eyes are so similar to her father's, there's no mistaking they're related. She skips alongside him, her smile lighting up the whole rink.

I straighten as I once again look to the man. I know better than to believe in coincidences. My eyes narrow as he stops a few feet from the counter. "Please tell me Holly didn't send you here."

Confusion contorts his features. "I beg your pardon?"

I blink. "Holly. She didn't..." My voice trails off, and my face flushes with scorching heat. "I'm so sorry."

He stands there, still looking confused.

Clearing my throat, I glance down at the little girl, then back to her father. "Hello," I say smoothly—professionally. "What can I do for you?" It's not enough to wipe away my mortification. I know better than to make assumptions, and yet I've done just that.

He takes a step closer, his features smoothing with more confidence and self-control than I will ever have. He taps a leather-gloved finger on one of the flyers I left on the counter. "I'd like to sign my daughter up for lessons." His voice has a warm timbre. The accent isn't something I can place despite traveling the world when I'd been a professional skater. It sends pleasant shivers down my spine, and I glance down at the flyer to steady myself.

This is not the time to get weak-kneed over a stranger. I have far more pressing issues to deal with. Holly will get a kick out of this when I tell her.

I nod and hunch over with my pencil poised. "Group lessons start tomorrow—"

"That's fine, but I want to inquire about additional private lessons."

My head snaps up, and my eyes lock with his once more. "I wasn't advertising private lessons—"

"I'm sure we can come to an arrangement that works in both our favors." Without missing a beat, he pulls out his checkbook.

I gawk at the thing. It's leather and has some kind of symbol embossed on its surface. He leans forward and retrieves a pen resting near my left hand. I jerk away before his glove can brush against me. Thankfully, he doesn't seem to notice.

With a flick of his wrist, he opens the booklet and gives me an expectant stare.

My mouth goes dry. "But I'm not..." A small voice in my head screams for me to take advantage. Clearly, he's well off. Based on his wardrobe, I wouldn't be surprised to discover he comes from old money. He wants the lessons, and I've known enough rich people to understand money doesn't mean much to them. I can probably name my price, and he'll scribble it onto that check right now.

I'm not a greedy person. I would never request something that isn't reasonable. And yet, that small voice grows louder still. "I suppose I could do thirty-minute sessions once a week—"

"Hour sessions. Three times weekly."

My eyes widen, and I suck in a breath. I cough once. Twice. "I'm sorry?"

He's already writing something on the check. "I want three lessons a week. One hour each."

My eyes dart to the small girl. "I'm not sure she can handle—"

"Annabelle is more than capable. Start out slow if you must—"

Irritation simmers in my blood. "If she's never skated before, she'll need to build her stamina. There are muscles to consider—"

He shoots me a look that makes me want to punch him in the face. If his daughter wasn't gazing at me with so much sincere curiosity, I might have done it anyway. He tears the check from his book and pushes it across the counter. "I'll be here for the month. I'm certain this will suffice."

My eyes drop to the check and my knees buckle. Two thousand dollars. My first name is scrawled on the top line, his almost regal signature at the bottom. *Kasper Montgomery*. I shove the check toward him so swiftly it lifts in the air and drops to the floor. "I can't," I stammer.

Kasper's brows furrow, and something flashes in his eyes. "Is it not enough?"

I gape. "It's too much."

At some point during my outburst, his daughter retrieves the check and returns it to the counter. I stare at the check like it's a predator ready to strike.

He relaxes and returns his checkbook to the inside of his suit coat. "Nonsense." Kasper says it like he's used to ordering people around. He probably is.

I clench my jaw, not willing to make a bigger fool of myself. I know I won't win an argument short of telling him I have the right to refuse service to anyone. Kasper's daughter peers at me with excitement, and I know I can't do that to her. Once more, I let my gaze sweep over the check, lingering on those zeros. That money would make a big dent in what I need.

I feel my defenses crumbling. "When would you like to start?"

Kasper glances around the empty rink. Technically, the free skating time doesn't start until evening. Usually, I'm in the middle of paperwork or preparations for opening. If I'd just had the good sense to lock the door behind me, I wouldn't be in this mess.

I also wouldn't be a few inches away from two grand.

"Today."

I stiffen. "Today? Are you—"

His gaze delves into mine. "Is that a problem?"

"Well, no, but—"

He removes his coat and slings it over his arm. Then he turns to his daughter. "I'll be sitting in the bleachers. You make sure to listen to Ms. Scarlett."

She nods resolutely, clearly raised to respect her teachers. I can't help the awe that slips past my defenses. As nervous as I am to pick up that check and commit to what Kasper wants me to do, I know it will be easy money—something I'm desperately in need of.

I place my fingers on the check and slide it toward me. His eyes are on me, but I don't risk looking up at him. I can't. If I do, I know I'll be trapped in those brown pools of power.

Power.

I need to be careful. People of power always take. They're never the sort to care about others. Case in point—he managed to get me to agree to something I'm not prepared to do. When he walks away, I lean over the counter, my forearms propping me up as I gaze at the sweet thing standing before me.

She stands tall and confident—much like her father. Her hands rest at her sides, and she lifts her chin so I can get a good look at her. I smile, and she smiles back. "Do you know what shoe size you are, sweetheart?"

The girl glances over her shoulder toward her father, then back to me before shaking her head.

I motion to her feet. "Let me see one of your shoes, and I'll get you a pair of skates."

Immediately, she drops to the floor and pulls a shoe from one foot, then the other. She stands and hands both of them to me. I don't get a chance to say anything before she all but bursts with excitement. "I've never been skating before. Daddy says I get to learn while we're visiting, and if I'm any good, then we can get me some skates when we get home."

Absentmindedly, I murmur, "Where are you from?"

"Averna."

My brows crease, and I glance up at her. "I've never heard of that place before." I expected her to mention something overseas like London or Britain.

She shrugs at my statement, not offering anything more. I reach under the counter and retrieve a pair of skates I know will fit her, then I walk out from behind the counter. Motioning toward a bench is all I have to do for her to take a seat. She swings her legs while I loosen the laces. Then she waits patiently while I strap her in.

"Is that too tight?"

"No," she says quietly.

"What's your name?" I finish tying the last one and get to my feet.

"Annabelle."

"That's a lovely name. Now, we're going to walk to the rink. Your legs are going to be a little wobbly while you get used to these. They're going to feel heavy and awkward. You can hold my hand if you need to."

She scoots to the edge of the bench and slips to the floor. Just as I predicted, her arms shoot out and her hands grip onto mine. She wobbles, unsure the first few steps, but quickly catches on.

We reach the edge of the ice, and I smile down at her. "I just ran the Zamboni. It's going to be really slick out there, but don't get nervous. It's okay if you fall down a few times. It's okay if you fall down a lot," I laugh. "The most important part is that you get back up. Listen to your body."

Annabelle tilts her head and scrunches her nose. "How do I do that?"

"Pay attention to the way your muscles move, how the ice feels beneath your skates, what your body wants to do to maintain your balance. Today that's all we're going to work on."

She nods, her courage evident. Then she steps out on the ice. Her hands flail, but she doesn't immediately crash to her bottom. Small skating movements are all she can muster, and I stay close by.

Again, I feel Kasper's stare on us. He's likely watching his daughter, but I certainly sense his attention more than I probably should. Annabelle has a natural ability to stay on her feet. I almost ask her if she's done gymnastics or other sports, but I keep my curiosity to myself.

By the end of our hour, Annabelle is exhausted. Surprisingly, she doesn't breathe a single complaint. I don't know whether to be impressed or worried. Powerful people tend to raise their children in such a way that demands they give it their all. I only glance at Kasper once while unlacing Annabelle's skates. "She did very well for her first time."

He nods as if nothing less would have been accepted, then he hands Annabelle her shoes.

"Is there a specific time that works best for lessons? My mornings are usually open."

Kasper glances around the rink. "Are you available around this time?"

It's late morning. The schedule would offer me time to see Holly for coffee in the morning if I need a good pick-me-up. I nod.

"We'll see you in two days," Kasper clips. He reaches for Annabelle's hand.

Her legs buckle briefly when her feet hit the floor. Kasper scoops her into his arms and turns toward the door. As cold as he is, I can't deny he adores his daughter. Annabelle grins at me and waves. "Bye, Miss Scarlett."

I wave back. When they're out of sight, I collapse onto the bench, emotionally spent.

Chapter 4

KASPER

Two days felt like an eternity. From the second I left Ice Castle, I couldn't stop thinking about her.

Scarlett.

I still don't know her last name. I don't dare ask that Holly woman, who seems to enjoy writing in the mornings at the same booth every day. I refuse to make any inquires that will draw attention to my interest.

There's something about Scarlett I can't put my finger on. I'm drawn to her as if something in the universe is telling me I need to be near her. But that's ridiculous and I know it.

The bench is cold beneath me, biting through the slacks I wear today. On the rink, Scarlett is teaching Annabelle how to lengthen her strides without falling over. She's done that more during this lesson than her last one.

My focus remains glued to the woman teaching my daughter. She's petite, with the body of a dancer. Blonde hair is pulled back from her face, showing off her delicate bone structure. I wouldn't be surprised to find out she was a ballet dancer in another life. It's the grace and poise she has that keeps me riveted—so different from what I would expect the owner of this sort of establishment to have.

I let my focus drift to the old skating rink. It's sturdy, but it could use some upgrades. I've been to hockey games where the ceiling is completely made from panes of glass so the night sky shines down on those skating. Those same rinks have a means to block out the sun for games played during the middle of the day. I wonder how hard it would be to make such an upgrade here.

When I look to the rink again, I find her staring at me. Her skin is paler, her eyes more defiant than usual. I stiffen. I've only interacted with Scarlett a handful of times. During each one, she's shown that she's more than capable of handling herself. But the look she's giving me now indicates she's offended by something—more specifically, something I've done.

I can't think of anything that would get her riled up. The fact that she hasn't broken her stare makes me wonder if I should be retreating. I lift my chin and keep my expression schooled. I won't let her intimidate me. I don't let anyone do that.

The second the lesson is over and Annabelle is situated on a bench to remove her shoes, Scarlett strides toward me with purpose. I rise, coat in hand, waiting for whatever it is she feels entitled to demand.

She places her hands on her hips, and her eyes narrow.

I bite back a smile. She doesn't know how to say what she wants to express. I cock my head to the side, my eyes sliding to where Annabelle is painstakingly unlacing her first skate. "Is there something you need, Ms. Scarlett?"

Her lips thin, and she glances over her shoulder to Annabelle. "I think you owe me an explanation."

I lift a single brow but don't say anything.

She lets out a sigh. "Aren't you going to tell me? I think it would be good for me to know…"

"My apologies, but I haven't the faintest clue about which you're speaking."

She moves closer. "Who you are."

My body stills, and my muscles grow tight. There's no way she knows who I am. No possible way. My gaze shifts to Annabelle, and I stifle a groan. Unless my daughter has something to do with it. I roll my shoulders back and flash her a smile. "I'm just a guy who wants his daughter to learn how to skate."

Scarlett scoffs. "And what about Annabelle's mother?"

What is she trying to imply? Is this what Annabelle said to bother her teacher? A low, rumbling irritation moves through me at that thought, and I speak through gritted teeth. "I don't see how it's any of your business, but my wife passed away nearly a year ago."

Brief surprise flitted across her face. Either Annabelle hadn't spilled that part, or she made some confusing statement about not having a mother. Likely the latter.

Scarlett brushes a hand over her hair, her face bleeding with color as a blush spreads beneath her skin. She brings her thumb to her lips, and her expression is more concerned than anything else. Her voice lowers, and she inches closer to me. "Annabelle said some things..." she hedged, "and I feel they're things I should have been made aware of—for insurance purposes."

My eyes narrow, though my frustration has officially fizzled out. "Well, what is it?"

Her blush deepens, making her eyes shine with a brighter intensity. She looks away, but her words are crystal clear. "Are you a king?"

I stare at her, unsure of whether I should laugh or march over to my daughter and reprimand her. We've gone over the rules. She isn't to tell a single soul who she is for her own safety. For the safety of us both. I fold my arms beneath my coat and let out a humorless chuckle. "If I were a king, do you think I'd be here without security?"

Her eyes widen, then her lashes flutter. I didn't think she could blush more than she has, but she's proving me wrong in the best way. "I—well I hadn't thought—" She frowns, and her eyes drop momentarily before she meets my gaze once more. "So, Annabelle isn't a princess," she mutters flatly.

"My daughter is very much a princess of Averna." I can't believe I'm actually telling her this. Normally I'd brush off her words and tell her to mind her own business. And yet here I stand, giving her the information I promised not only myself but my parents that I wouldn't share.

The confusion that paints her face is almost enough to cover up her embarrassment. "But you said—"

I drag a hand down my face. "My *father* is the king. I'm a prince. Annabelle is a princess."

"And you're going to be a king one day?"

"I sure hope not." I blurt out the words without hesitation.

Her head rears back and her lips part as if prepared to ask another question, but she stops herself—probably the smartest thing she's done since confronting me.

I know there's no getting out of this conversation. Americans are too nosy for their own good. Breathing out a sigh through pursed lips, I rake my fingers through my hair. "My brother is next in line for the throne. It's none of your business, but I'm behind my brother and his children—when he has them." I watch a myriad of emotions flicker across her face. It's not every day someone meets a member of a royal family. We're not a big enough country to warrant being known, anyway. Still, my irritation has peaked, and I'm ready to be done with this conversation. "If we're done with this interrogation, I'd like to take my daughter home." I move to step away, then pause and look at her. "And I'd appreciate your discretion in this matter." I brush past her, almost giving into guilt for being so curt with her. There's no reason she needs my life story—royal background or no.

I sense more than hear her spin around to face my direction. She doesn't argue. She doesn't even call out to me. The conversation is over, and I anticipate she won't bring it up again. For now, I need to have a much-needed conversation with my daughter.

WE SIT OUTSIDE IN THE COLD ON A WOODEN BENCH. Behind us is a small candy shop. Stella's seems to be the place everyone goes out of their way to visit. Even people in the airport mentioned the shop.

I expected to find a shop like all the others—filled with truffles, candied apples, and fudge. Never in my wildest dreams did I believe a small town in Idaho would have a candy shop with treats suited to our tastes.

I hold a clear bag with a scoop of sugar plums. The hard candy wasn't something I thought the States enjoyed, but I was wrong. Shoving my hand into the bag, I glance at Annabelle, who's happily sucking on a pink candy cane. She glances up at me, then frowns.

She knows what's about to happen.

Sighing, I shift so I can place my arm around her shoulder. "You shouldn't have told Ms. Scarlett you're a princess."

"Why not? All my other teachers know."

I know this is going to be a difficult discussion. "Because we're not in Averna. We didn't bring any of our security. It's a secret we're here."

Her frown deepens.

I try to come up with a reasonable explanation, but the only thing I can think of to say is, "Do you like having security follow us everywhere? To have them check every room before we walk in? I thought you didn't like when you had to follow their rules."

Slowly, she shakes her head. Her hand holding the candy cane falls to her lap. "No."

"That's why we're keeping it a secret. If no one knows where we are or who we are, then we can have a break." I'm not about to tell her I'm still hyper-vigilant when it comes to our safety. I want her to have one month where she can be like everyone else.

"Okay." Her quiet mumble tugs at my heart.

"But I guess since Miss Scarlett knows, you can tell her whatever you'd like."

The bright smile returns to my daughter's face, and she resumes eating her candy cane. I pop a sugar plum into my mouth and crunch down on its sweet-nutty flavor. My daughter swings her legs, quickly bouncing back from the quiet chastisement I subjected her to.

My thoughts shift to Scarlett and the reaction she had to that short exchange. I have to admit it's smart of her to be concerned about the liability involved with having us on site—with no security. It makes me wonder if she's been in situations where people got hurt.

I brush off that thought as soon as it appears. Not only should we be keeping our status a secret, we need to keep to ourselves in general. I can't allow myself to develop an interest in her. We'll be leaving in a month's time. I'm here to get closer to my daughter as we near the anniversary of her mother's death.

Glancing down at her beside me, I breathe in deeply, then let the air out in a white puff. Annabelle is my whole world, and she will continue to be so. She will never have to worry about losing me—not to anything or anyone.

Chapter 5

SCARLETT

It's completely illogical, and I know it. But something isn't sitting right in my stomach. Kasper Montgomery is a prince. A real-life prince. Flesh and blood. I place my head in my hand as I sit at my desk. Why can't I accept it and move on?

That part of me refusing to let it go has me nearly convinced to give him back his money and tell him to look elsewhere. I don't have time in my life for drama. I need to figure out how to raise the rest of the money because lessons aren't cutting it. The last thing I need is for this information to leak and the press to come around asking questions.

Is Kasper the prince of a well-known country? No. But he's still a prince. The paparazzi have been riled up for less.

It's not just the fact that he's royalty, I remind myself. It's the principle of the thing. I was being honest when I told him it was about keeping Annabelle safe. My rink is far from secure. I've come into work before to find the drawers rifled through. Unfortunately, I don't make enough to get much more than a living wage from running the place. The cost for upkeep is just too great.

I ease back into my desk chair and twist it side to side. My concerns are valid, and no one is going to tell me otherwise. My eyes drift to the phone on my desk, and my fingers twitch. It's been twenty-four hours since I found out, and I'm still just as anxious. I need to tell someone. But Kasper asked me to stay quiet.

The phone remains dark, but I can feel the urge grow within me. There's only one person I can tell who wouldn't breathe a word. She's married to a famous person, too. She'll understand the need for secrecy. And perhaps Holly will have a perspective that will help me.

I snatch the phone off my desk and dial her number.

"Hello?"

"Coffee?"

"I can be there in twenty."

I smile as we both hang up without another word. Holly is a godsend. I moved here before she did, but I never connected with anyone. After the issues with my manager, I don't know that I ever will again.

Thinking about what Kevin did to me leaves a bitter taste in my mouth. A visit with a friend is just what the doctor ordered. It takes only ten minutes to lock up and start on my way to the coffee shop. I receive my order from the barista as a happy female voice behind me chastises, "You should have waited. It's supposed to be my treat."

I turn with both cups in hand, chagrined. "Sorry."

Though Holly's eyes are bright and happy, her lips thin to a disapproving frown. "Seriously, Scarlett. You're literally trying to save your rink. You shouldn't be spending money—"

"Okay, alright. I know." I shove the cup into her hands. "I invited you. I thought I should pay."

I can tell she wants to tell me to reconsider her offer for help with my bills. As much as I want to give in, I can't. Thankfully, she doesn't voice her desire, saving me from having to turn her down yet again. Holly lifts the coffee and tilts her head, concern now the forefront of her expression. "What's going on? More bad news?"

I grimace. "Not in the way you'd think." Glancing around, I take note of those in the crowded coffee shop. Cup of Joy is always busy. I can't think of a single time of day when there aren't at least a couple people enjoying the quiet ambiance and the smell of those delicious coffee beans. "Can we take a walk? I know it's freezing outside, but I..." My eyes plead with her. I can't risk anyone else overhearing what I have to tell her.

For a moment, I falter. Kasper asked for my discretion. But I can trust Holly. And I need to work a few things out. I push away the hesitation and jerk my head toward the door.

"Please?"

The crease in her brows deepens, and she nods. "Yeah. Sure."

Our shoes crunch into the crisp snow and salt that lines the pavement. The sun is shining, making every crystal glisten. A man dressed as Santa is already ringing a bell outside the grocery store at the end of the road, the jingling sound drawing my attention. This used to be my favorite time of year, and now all I can think about is how everything continues to go wrong at every turn.

"Okay," Holly drawls, "what's going on? I've never seen you this antsy. Not even when Kevin…" Her voice trails off.

My head aches, and my chest heaves. "What I'm going to tell you—I don't want you to breathe a word of it to anyone. Not even Lucian."

She gives me a look—one that says I know I can't ask her to keep things from her husband.

I groan. "It's not a bad thing. I don't think Lucian would even care."

Still, she lifts a brow.

"Fine, if you have to tell him, then… whatever. But we can't share it beyond that." I suck in a deep breath, then face my friend. "Kasper is a prince."

She stares at me for a moment, her face blank. Then a laugh bursts from her lips. "You're kidding."

My expression remains frozen, and she sobers.

"You're kidding, right?"

Slowly, I shake my head. "It's some small country I've never heard of, but I looked it up. He's telling the truth."

Holly gasps, reaching for my upper arm and dragging me to the side of the street. "A real live prince? What is he doing here? In Breckenridge of all places?"

I shrug. "He didn't say. All he said was that… he wants my discretion."

"How did you find out? Did he tell you?"

Shaking my head, my irritation rises. "That's just it. I wouldn't have known if his daughter didn't say something. I don't think she was supposed to." I let out a huff. "He's a jerk, right? He should have told me. I needed to know what I was dealing with."

Holly gives me a side-eyed look. "Not necessarily..." she murmurs.

My mouth drops open. "Absolutely he should have! It's a matter of principle. What if he draws unwanted attention—dangers." I whisper the last word. Based on the look Holly wears, I can tell she thinks I'm reaching. I want to stomp my foot and fold my arms, but I can't with the coffee in hand. "There's liability to consider," I mutter in a last-ditch effort.

"Are you..." She presses her lips together as if she needs a moment to choose her words carefully. "Maybe you're upset because of Kevin."

I gasp. "How can you say that? They have nothing in common!"

She shrugs. "Kevin burned you. He lied to your face and left you to pick up the pieces. Kasper? He's a stranger. He doesn't owe you anything. Just because you found out something about him that he didn't plan on telling you doesn't mean he's betraying your trust. He paid you to teach his kid. That's it. There's nothing else." A sly smile slips across her face. "Unless you want more..."

"Oh, shut up," I mutter.

"I mean it, Scarlett. Who wouldn't want a prince to come in on a white horse and sweep her off her feet? Maybe this is exactly what you need."

I gape at her. She's officially gone crazy. "The man is a prince, Holly! He's here for a month before he returns home to his country to do whatever princes do."

"Become king?" she says wryly.

I wave a hand through the air. "No. His brother's going to be king. I don't know what his responsibilities are."

Holly's amusement grows with each statement I make. She tilts her head, her eyes dancing. "Keep an open mind. You never know what could change."

※ ※ ※

Kasper and Annabelle show up for her lesson right on time. I'm standing behind the counter, pouring over the documents. I have so many bills. So many threats to shut off utilities if I don't send them something. Holly was right in chastising me about buying coffee—I simply can't afford it.

Two small hands land on the counter, and I glance up to see Annabelle grinning at me. "What are you doing?" she asks as she peers up over the counter.

I pull the documents closer to myself and shove them beneath a stack of flyers. Pasting on my best smile, I lean over so she can see me better. "I'm getting a few things ready for a party." Holly had come up with the idea after I vented to her about my issues with Kasper. She had practically brushed them away like they were a pesky fly. I know she made a good point, but I can't bring myself to look at the man without seeing the lies.

My eyes lift to his where he stands behind his daughter, then I drop them to Annabelle once again. I'll ignore him. He paid me to teach his daughter, not to befriend him.

Annabelle's eyes brighten at my answer. "A party?"

I nod. "I'm going to have a big skate night to raise some extra money." Without even looking at the imposing figure a few feet away, I can sense the way he stiffens. He doesn't know about my financial issues, and I have no intention of telling him. Any assumption he makes is on him.

"What are you going to do?" Annabelle asks. "Will there be music?"

I laugh despite myself. "Of course there will be music. And food and games and prizes." I've made up my mind to ask some of the businesses in town for donations. I'm praying they won't ask too many questions, either. I'm still new, but the folks in and around Breckenridge seem to look out for their own. Besides, it's not like they're just giving something for nothing. Being showcased means having their name out there, and more potential customers.

Annabelle jumps up and down, then spins around to look at her father. "Can we go? Please?"

As if against my own will, my eyes lift to meet his. I stand straighter, knowing I can't tell him I'd prefer he stays away. He glances to me, and his eyes lock on my face. Without turning to his daughter, he says, "Of course, bug. Sounds like fun."

I do my best to quash my disappointment as I turn a bright smile on my pupil. "Let's get you laced up, okay?" I reach for the skates I have waiting for her and hand them over the counter. "Can you get them on, and I'll be right over there to help you lace them?"

Annabelle scoops the skates into her arms and hurries toward the bench we usually sit on.

Kasper is still standing in front of my counter.

I pull the documents from where I hid them and double-check the numbers. "Do you need something, Mr. Montgomery?"

My eyes lift to meet his. "Or should I say your *highness*?" My tone is bitter.

He's looking at the documents in front of me, and I place both hands on them, drawing his gaze to meet mine. He stares at me expectantly as if he didn't hear what I said.

"Did you need something?" I ask again.

Kasper motions to the stack of flyers. "The party is this weekend?"

I don't deign an answer.

"I'd like to help pass them out."

My refusal clings to my tongue, but I know that it wouldn't matter what I say. Something tells me's going to pester me until I let him do something. It probably has a lot to do with his royal status. I doubt many have told him no and lived to tell the tale. My eyes narrow, and I sigh. "Fine. I'm going to pass them out after Annabelle's lesson." I give him a look—one I hope he understands to mean run along now. Thankfully, he nods and then turns for his usual spot on the bleachers.

Chapter 6

KASPER

I don't know why it bothers me that Annabelle's ice-skating teacher dislikes me so much. It's not like we were friends when I signed up for her lessons, but there's a distinct coldness coming from her that irritates me.

It's like an itch that can't be scratched. It's a facial twitch or hiccups that last too long. I refuse to accept that my perception has anything to do with the fact that people in Averna are more than respectful toward me. And I won't be staying past the holiday, so it really shouldn't matter.

And yet.

It goes back to those first few days after I'd met her. I could sense something about her that was so compelling I couldn't take my eyes off her no matter how hard I tried. She was a creature of beauty, but it was more than that.

I shake off my musings and focus on the stack of flyers in my hand. Meredith was more than happy to keep an eye on Annabelle when she didn't want to be out in the cold today. I think it has more to do with her finding the games under the stairs at The Gingerbread Cottage than anything else.

It's a colder day today. The sky is overcast with grey clouds, and a gentle breeze lowers the temperature further. It hasn't snowed since my arrival, but I'm hoping it will. We get few snowy days back home, and when we do, it never sticks to the ground. That's the biggest reason for my picking this snowy town. Everyone should experience the magic of Christmas, snow included.

Scarlett's footsteps crunch along with my own. The wind picks up and ruffles the pages in my hands. I duck my head a little lower against the chill and risk a quick look at the woman beside me. Her jaw is set and her eyes are determined—but I read more than her dislike for me there.

My gaze dips to the flyers. She needs to raise money. Does that mean her business is struggling? It wouldn't be a surprise considering how small the town is. How often do people go skating throughout the year?

A question forms on my lips, but I stamp it out. It's none of my business what she's going through. We have a professional arrangement, and it will remain as such.

I just want her to stop looking at me like I'm the villain in her story.

Everyone in this town has been kind. Even the few interactions I've had with Holly have gone well. Scarlett is the only one who—

"What?" Her voice jerks me out of my thoughts. It's the first thing she's said to me since we left the bed and breakfast.

I stiffen. "I didn't say anything."

She rolls her eyes. "You're staring."

Am I? I can feel the heat of embarrassment flood my insides, threatening to rise and show itself all over my face. I avert my gaze and shake my head. "It wasn't my intention."

A huff bursts from her lips, the cloud puffing in the air between us as we stop in front of the coffee shop. Something flickers across her features that I can only assume is disappointment. But as quickly as it appears, it's gone. "You go in there and give them the flyer. I'm going across the street to the bookstore." She marches in that direction, and my gaze bounces from her to the coffee shop and back.

Does she want a hot drink? I wouldn't mind one for myself. The cold is sinking into my body, being absorbed by my very bones. And I'm sure my layers are warmer than her jeans and down coat.

I push into the coffee shop, and heat wraps its expansive arms around me. Without pausing for even a moment, I march up to the front counter. The woman behind the counter, Jess, smiles broadly at me.

Holding out the flyer, I flash her a smile as well. "Scarlett over at the ice-skating rink is hosting a skate night. She wants to get the word out."

Jess takes the flyer, her eyes sweeping over the words. Her smile deepens. "This sounds like so much fun." Her eyes meet mine. "Can I take a few of those? I can leave them on the tables."

I nod and hand them to her. "We're also asking if the local businesses would like to donate anything for the raffles." I motion to the several people who are currently enjoying lunch at the tables. "I'm sure people would love to win a gift card to this place."

Jess nibbles on her lip, tilting her head as she glances around the room. "I suppose I can give you a few. One moment while I ring them up."

"Also, I'd like to make a purchase."

She nods. "Sure. What can I get for you?"

Thumbing over my shoulder, I say, "Scarlett... what does she like?"

"She doesn't have a usual. But she does seem to like anything with caramel in it."

I grin. "Make it two."

Jess smiles and nods again.

"Oh, and a gift card for me as well."

"How much?"

"One hundred."

She blinks and glances at me as if she doesn't believe she heard me correctly. Then she types the amount into her tablet and turns it to face me. "That's one-hundred-ten dollars and fifteen cents."

I pull out my card and make sure to leave her a tip, then stand to the side while she makes the drinks. Once the coffees are complete, she slides an envelope across the counter. "There are five gift cards in there for five dollars each. Tell Scarlett I'll be there."

I pocket the envelope and the gift card I purchased. Then I scoop up my flyers into one arm and grab the coffees with my free hand.

Scarlett is outside waiting when I emerge. Her irritation fades to surprise when she sees the drinks. Her gaze jumps up to meet mine, smoothing into a mask of unreadability. "You got coffee." It isn't a question.

"One is for you," I offer.

She doesn't move right away to take it. Instead, she eyes it like something is going to jump right out of the cup and bite her. "What is it?"

I shrug. "Something caramel. Jess seemed to think you'd like it."

"Which one is mine?"

I push the cup carrier toward her. "They're the same thing. Just take one, will you?"

She shoots me an incredulous look but accepts the beverage.

Shoving the pages under my arm, I pull the cup from the cardboard carrier before tossing the latter in a nearby garbage can.

Scarlett sips her drink as we continue down the street to the next shop. Her steps are slower this time, and she keeps glancing at me. "Thank you," she finally whispers.

"Jess donated five gift cards to your raffle too."

She blinks. "Oh. I totally forgot to remind you…"

"You didn't have to." I give her a nod, hoping she interprets it to mean we've got similar goals—though I'm still not sure what her endgame is.

Her expression clouds over all the same, and I sigh.

"What is your problem?"

This time she jumps and stares at me like I've slapped her across the face. "What?"

"Clearly you despise me."

She scowls this time. "I don't know what you're talking about."

"Yes, you do. You barely talk to me unless you absolutely have to. I saw that look in your eyes when I offered to help—you'd rather fling yourself off the nearest mountain before spending any time in my company."

She scoffs. "I don't know what it's like where you come from, but here, tourists don't try to forge friendships."

"I'm not trying to forge any such thing," I grind out. "But I would also appreciate a bit more respect."

We stop in the middle of the sidewalk, and she whirls to face me. "Respect? Is that what you call barging into my rink and demanding skating lessons that I don't offer? Is that what you call it when you leave out specific details about who you are and what you do?"

I want to drag my hand down my face, but between the coffee and the flyers, I can't. Instead, I step closer to her. She doesn't retreat. Surprisingly, she lifts her chin, and her eyes flash with fire. When I don't say anything, she huffs with derision.

"I'm an owner of a rink in a town you are visiting. I'm busy—I have to plan as many of these skate nights this month as I can, and I don't have time to placate a spoiled prince."

The words slip out of my mouth before I know what I'm saying. "Then I'll be at every single one of them until you admit that you don't like me."

"Of course I don't like you. Not everyone has to like you." She rolls her eyes and continues down the sidewalk, forcing me to rush to catch up.

"Why not?"

She shakes her head. "Why doesn't everyone have to like you? Gee you really are sheltered, aren't you?"

"Why don't *you* like me?" I snap back.

Scarlett stops again and faces me. "Because you're a liar. You hide things about yourself, which I find off-putting and sketchy."

My brows lift. "That's it? You find out one thing about me that you didn't know and now you want my life story? Fine. I'll tell you. I'm the middle child of three. All brothers. My oldest brother is next in line for the throne, and he's been trained and taught his whole life. My baby brother is the favorite. Everyone loves him—he'd probably be a better option for king one day, but that's just not how it goes."

Her eyes widen as I continue to ramble.

"I married young—she was my high school sweetheart, and my parents loved her. It was a fairytale sort of love. But she died in a car accident just before Annabelle's first birthday."

Scarlett gasped but didn't interrupt.

"I came here to get away from the prying eyes and the pitying looks I still get, even though it's been almost four years since her passing. My responsibilities are more for show than anything else—partly to do with my position in the family, and partly because of what I've lost." My chest is heaving as I continue to spill everything she probably doesn't care to hear.

People passing are giving us strange looks, but I don't care anymore. It's as if opening these flood gates is exactly what my heart needs—has needed since Rose was ripped from my life.

"Before Annabelle was born, I loved reading, the outdoors, and travel. Now, she's my whole world. I would do anything to make sure she's happy, and that's the other reason we're here. She's never seen a real snowfall—not one where she can lie in it and make snow angels or have a snowball fight." My last few words hang in the air between us until I finally say, "Is that enough information for you? I have nothing to hide—I just happen to be a private person who doesn't particularly like it when I'm being judged for something I haven't done."

Her only response is to blink at me. Then her cheeks flush, and she looks away. "I'm sorry," she murmurs. Scarlett's eyes lift to meet mine, and her blush deepens.

My tirade has put a different wall up between us, and I'm not sure it's any better. I want to apologize as well, but I keep my mouth shut.

She nods her head toward the toy store currently across the street. "Should we..."

I glance in that direction and nod. "Yeah. Sure. Let's go."

Chapter 7

SCARLETT

I'm an idiot. That's all I can think about throughout the week as I make my preparations for the skate night. Every time I close my eyes. Every time I find a spare minute to breathe, that conversation comes back to me.

I was mortified. He probably saw that the second he finished his rant. And like a gentleman, he didn't rub it in.

I groan, placing my face in my hands before scrubbing them free. It's so embarrassing that I let my bad mood and my stubbornness get in the way of seeing what an actual good guy the prince truly is.

There's no telling how long I'll have to live with this embarrassment. Probably forever—definitely longer than he plans to be in Breckenridge.

My gaze shifts to the rink. It's too early for people to be arriving, and it lays empty. The ice practically glows beneath the lighting overhead. It calls to me, but I have too much left to do before I open the doors. The raffle items are spread out before me, waiting for me to label them. With each item, I have a clear jar and a roll of tickets. Some raffles will be one dollar. Others a bit more. I'm hoping people will enter several of them.

The tightness in my stomach worsens. I wonder if it would benefit me more to tell everyone why I'm doing this fundraiser of sorts. I hadn't been bad with my money. I didn't gamble it all away or lose it in a bet.

I just bet on the wrong guy to take care of it.

Embarrassment from that knowledge mingles with that of how I treated Kasper.

His name carries a different kind of weight in my chest, and my thoughts shift to him.

For all intents and purposes, the man is perfect. He always dresses nice. He's good with his daughter. He's respectful to a fault.

I groan again, this time letting a growl come with it.

Kasper is the opposite of what I tried to peg him as.

"Everything okay?" A low voice shatters the quiet around me.

I jump, my head snapping up to find the one person I'd rather not come face-to-face with. My eyes lock with his, and time slows. All the conversations I've had with Holly since his arrival come rushing back, and my heart ticks up several beats.

He's cute. Maybe you need to let him sweep you off your feet. You need a distraction.

I shake my head to clear it, and he frowns.

"Something wrong?" Kasper glances around the rink.

"No! Of course not," I say more gently. Heat sears my face, and I rise from the stool I'm sitting on. "Everything is on schedule for this evening." I gesture to the raffle items with a ridiculous flourish. "Just the finishing touches."

His hands are in the pockets of his long suit coat as he strolls closer to me. His eyes sweep over the countertop, and a wry smile graces his handsome face. "Looks like you made out like a bandit. I don't remember this much being donated when we put up flyers."

I swallow hard. "It wasn't. Some of it trickled in." I hate how small my voice sounds, how unsure of myself I've suddenly become in his presence.

He can tell. I know he senses how the power dynamics have changed, and I hate him for that, too.

Dumb. It's not his fault I put my foot in my mouth far too many times.

Kasper glances up at me once more, and I flash him a nervous smile. Then my eyes shift away, seeking out his shadow. "Is Annabelle not with you?"

He tilts his head, and that smile is almost enough to make me melt where I stand. "I asked Meredith to keep an eye on her. She was busy doing some puzzles, and I didn't want to pull her away while I came here."

"Why?" I blink several times. "I mean, why *are* you here?"

"I thought I could help with those finishing touches." His voice is smooth and soft. It's like the first step into a perfectly hot bath on a cold December night.

I shiver, then attempt to shake off the feelings. "You've already done enough." More than enough. He not only helped with the flyers, he helped with the more than generous payment he made for Annabelle's lessons. Without that inflow of cash, I wouldn't be able to keep the lights on.

Instead of arguing with me, he removes his coat and drapes it over the edge of the counter. "We're preparing the raffles, right? Looks like you're writing what the prize is and how much each ticket is worth?" He picks up a roll of tickets to examine it, and I can't stop myself from reaching out to snatch it back. Kasper is too quick. He holds it over his head and grins that devil-may-care smile.

I settle back on my feet with a thump, no longer on my toes. "*We're* not preparing anything. You don't have to be here."

"Think of it as me donating my time."

My eyes narrow, and that thumping in my chest grows more erratic. I can't be here with him alone. It's more than the embarrassment. It's Holly's teasing words.

Let him sweep you off your feet.

Kasper isn't leaving, though. I know it better than I know this rink. He confirms my suspicions when he says, "I have it on good authority that you're letting that nice woman from Stella's donate her time—and her goodies." He's not wrong. I don't know how he knows this, but it really doesn't matter.

I heave a sigh and twirl my hand. "Fine. Do whatever you want." I avoid looking directly at him. Too much to do. And even though I now have someone helping, I don't know if I'll have even a spare second before skaters start to arrive.

❄ ❄ ❄

"Scarlett," Holly is breathless when she arrives

at the counter where I stand. Her face is etched in worry. "The toilet is overflowing in the girl's bathroom."

"What?" I snap. The rink is filled with people. The whole town seems to have shown up for the skate night. Up until this moment, I thought everything was going to work out perfectly.

"I don't know if it was just one of those unfortunate situations or if someone intentionally clogged it, but the water is spilling over the basin."

Without a moment's hesitation, I dart around the counter. I shouldn't leave my space. If people arrive to skate, they'll have to wait for me to get back. I cast a lingering look at the counter. No one is available to man it right now. Eva is working at the concessions. Holly volunteered to keep an eye on the rink and surrounding bleachers for safety. I don't have anyone else.

The thought flits through my mind as I turn my focus forward and bump into a hard body. I gasp. "I'm so sorr—"

Kasper's warm hands are holding my upper arms, keeping me steady. He smiles at me, but it fades when he sees my expression. "Everything okay?"

"Yeah," I blush. "It's just an overflowing toilet. Nothing I can't handle."

His eyes shift to the counter behind me, and it's like he's thinking the same thing I am. His brows pull together with concern before his eyes catch mine again. "What can I do to help?"

I attempt to wave him off.

"Scarlett!" Holly calls.

My focus shifts to Holly then to Kasper. "There's nothing—"

He glances over to Holly, then he gives me a sharp nod. "You stay here. I can handle it."

"You—what? Wait!" My eyes are wide as he all but rushes after Holly. There's a maintenance closet between the two bathrooms. Holly's aware of it and it's unlocked. I know that between the two of them, they'll be able to handle the problem, but I still feel myself being tugged in their direction.

"Scarlett?" Someone calls my name, and I turn around to see Ivy standing at the counter. Her short, straight, black hair swishes with every movement she makes, and her almond eyes shine brighter than her smile.

I hurry toward her, praying the reporter doesn't need to use the restroom while she's here. I only know her from the handful of articles she's written about Breckenridge—the latest one being the most recent addition to the small town. Lucian Scott. Actor and owner of the local bed and breakfast.

Forcing a nervous smile, I ask, "What can I do for you?"

She motions to the wall of skates behind me. "How much for a pair of skates?"

A breath of relief leaves my lungs, and I set her up with a pair. "Have fun," I call after her.

When the last person says their goodbyes and leaves the rink, I sink onto the stool behind the counter. My hair is a frazzled mess. The rink is littered with raffle tickets and food wrappers despite Holly's best efforts to keep it clean. The Ice Castle rink hasn't been this busy ever. If I end up surviving until

January, then perhaps I'll need to incorporate at least one skate night a month.

Movement catches my attention, and Kasper emerges from the bathrooms on the far side of the rink. I jump to my feet and stride toward him. "What are you still doing here?"

His dress shirt sleeves are rolled up to his elbows, and his tie is gone. I've never seen his brown hair so disheveled. He's drop-dead gorgeous.

Thankfully, Kasper doesn't notice my stare. He thumbs over his shoulder. "Bathrooms are clean. What else can I do?"

My brain loses all functionality as I gape at him. He grins at me and waves a hand in my face. I blurt, "I thought you left with Annabelle."

"I asked Holly to take her back. Annabelle adores her."

All I can do is blink.

He motions again to the rink. "If you can't think of anything, I'll start picking up trash."

I want to stop him, to tell him a prince shouldn't be picking up garbage. But I can't find the words. Instead, I numbly start picking up the garbage with him. We work side by side for several minutes. I cast glances in his direction several times. Some sort of dam bursts inside me, and I spill everything I've been worried about.

"I'm not normally like this, you know."

He glances at me, and I flush.

"Angry all the time. Irritated all the time." I make a face. "Before..." Biting my lip and closing my eyes, I shake my head. "This place is my dream."

"It's a nice dream," he comments quietly.

"It is," I agree. "But not when it's about to be taken from you."

At the incredulous look on his face, I hurry to explain.

"I'm a little behind on my finances. I'm trying my best to fill in the gap." I let out a mirthless laugh. "I'm not even sure what I'm doing will help, but I have to do something." I'm not looking at him as I say it.

"Well, that's an easy fix."

My eyes dart to him. We've made it back to the counter where his coat still waits, and he's pawing through the pockets. I'm not sure what he's doing until I see that ridiculous checkbook appear.

"How behind are you?"

The numbness I've been feeling bursts with a hot, fiery rage. "Put that away," I bite out.

"I beg your pardon?" He looks genuinely confused.

"Money doesn't solve everything!" I spew the statement that I've said to myself several times over the years. Hard work. Determination. Only I can fix this and I won't allow myself to depend on anyone—not even a prince.

His features tighten, and he taps the checkbook on his palm. "In this case it does." His voice is hard—firm. I've only heard that tone once before, and I hate it even more this time.

My mouth drops open. Technically, he's right. But it's not the money itself that I'm upset with. I don't know what I'm upset about, actually. I just know I'm not going to let some stranger throw money at my problem. If I can't fix this myself, then I'm not worthy of having it.

"Thank you for the offer," I grind out, the words tearing at me, "but I'm not going to be your charity project."

"That's not—"

"Thank you for your help." This time I swing an arm toward the door, my voice pointed. "I'll see Annabelle for her lesson early next week."

His expression hardens, jaw ticking. I can see a familiar fire in his eyes—one that mirrors my own. For a moment, I wonder if he's going to argue with me, but he doesn't. He scoops his coat onto his arm and charges past me to the door.

Chapter 8

KASPER

Dang it all!

That woman has got to be the most stubborn person I have ever met. I'm seething, practically steaming outside as I stalk though the night toward The Gingerbread Cottage. I'm sure Annabelle is still up and waiting for me. I wouldn't expect Meredith to help with her bedtime routine. In fact, everyone at that bed and breakfast has been more than accommodating. I need to remember to tip them well before I leave.

My thoughts continue bouncing around my head without any purpose. I've never been so flustered in all my life, and it's got my teeth on edge.

I want to march right back to that ice skating rink and tell Scarlett that she doesn't have a choice. She'll accept my money and say thank you.

But she's not my subject. And I'm not a king.

By the time I make it to the path leading up to the entrance of the Gingerbread Cottage, I'm more worked up than ever. My phone vibrates in my pocket, and I grow still, not daring to hope that she'd actually call me to tell me I was right. My heart ticks up its speed, and I dig the darn thing from my pocket to find my brother's name on the ID.

I frown. It's the third missed call I've received from my younger brother. Admittedly, I've been avoiding speaking to my family since my arrival. None of them were happy about me missing our own festivities over the month of December, and all of them were more than irritated about not taking security with us.

But why would James be calling me?

My father has called once, but that was all.

Nothing from my mother. Nothing from Alexander.

My thumb hovers over the spot to answer the call, then I shake my head. I'm in no mood to speak to anyone who wants to criticize me.

I shove the phone into my pocket and make my way more slowly toward the front steps of the cottage. The exterior lights twinkle merrily, but they do nothing to improve my mood. The Christmas spirit I've been hoping to find seems to have fizzled out.

Several lights are still on inside. I can hear Christmas music playing, but I can't bring myself to go inside. Not yet.

Too many emotions are swirling inside me. Too many disappointments.

All my life, I've only wanted to be able to fix things—to help others. It was my small way to contribute to an otherwise depressing world. I wasn't going to lead my country. And I don't bring the sort of joy to my family that James does.

My one and only contribution is Annabelle. I married well. They all said as much. My folks adored my wife.

But now she's gone.

I couldn't save her. I can't bring her back. The car accident ripped her from our lives, and we're stuck with the hollow memory of her.

I place my head in my hands and rest my elbows on my knees. Being a prince, having wealth, it wasn't enough to keep ahold of that part of my life. But it can help Scarlett, and she refuses to accept it.

My mood shifts from exasperation to irritation. She's a fool. A stubborn fool who is too proud to accept the help from others. I'm not even a friend—practically a stranger—and she can't bring herself to let me help. Have her other friends tried?

I lift my head and glance at the windows to the cottage behind me. Has Holly tried?

It wouldn't surprise me in the least. But Holly doesn't seem like the sort of person who takes no for an answer.

I let out a sharp huff, but then another thought pops into my head. Perhaps her aversion to accepting help is because she's embarrassed that she made poor financial decisions. She doesn't want to accept my offer because she could fail again.

That realization hits me in the chest, and there is absolutely nothing I can do about it. Understanding washes over me, cooling my temper and giving me the peace I didn't know I needed. I can relate to that.

If Scarlett is determined to save her rink her way, so she feels confident running it in the future, who am I to take that away from her? I may not agree with her process, but I can respect it.

The relief and peace are short-lived as I contemplate how I left things only twenty minutes ago. Well, shoot. I've probably made the next couple of weeks even more miserable. And we were getting along so nicely. I'll have to figure out a way to apologize or accept the torture that is Scarlett's dark stare and cold shoulder.

I SHOVE MY HANDS INTO MY POCKETS AS I STRIDE DOWN the sidewalk with Annabelle at my side. She skips along, chatting about how much fun she's having with Meredith and how she reminds Annabelle of the housekeeper at home.

I smile, and my gaze lands on a bakery I've been wanting to visit again.

Stella's looks like it came straight out of a fairytale. The brick building is old but sturdy. The windows on either side of the door are large and brightly lit. Displays of goodies are spread out before anyone who happens to glance its way.

Annabelle notices too, and she hurries to the window to look. Her small hands press against the glass. She stares, mouth wide, at the new assortment of treats. "Can I get one?" she asks without looking up at me.

"You want another candy cane?"

She shakes her head and points to the candied apples. "I want one of those."

I chuckle. My mouth waters at the thought of getting more of those traditional sugar plums, but more options are being showcased. I stare down at the small sign beside what look to be cookies coated in a deep purple, sugary swirl. "Sugar plum inspired cookies," I muse aloud.

Annabelle glances briefly at the cookies, then shakes her head. "No. I want an apple."

I smile at her and nod. "Okay. Let's get you an apple. Do you think Miss Scarlett would like something too? Your lesson is in about twenty minutes." I've been trying to think of some way to make a peace offering, and money is definitely not the way to go.

As I expect, Annabelle nods with excitement. "Yeah! Let's get her a treat too." She lifts her hand to take mine, and I move to the door to push it open.

A woman is leaning over the counter, her forearms resting on its surface as she speaks to a man in a suit. I've seen the man around before, but I don't know who he is. The woman, though... I've met her.

She straightens and smiles broadly. "Kasper, isn't it?" Her eyes dip to Annabelle. "And cute little Annabelle."

My daughter beams with surprise. "You know my name?"

Eva's smile broadens. "Of course I do. How could I forget such a pretty little girl like you?" She reaches across the counter and pulls out a pink candy cane. "Are you here for more of this?"

Annabelle shakes her head. "I want a candy apple like the one in the window."

Eva glances over to the display, then tilts her head. "Of course." Her eyes flit up to meet mine. "And for you?"

"He wants the cookies," Annabelle comments without

waiting for me to answer. "And we want something special for Miss Scarlett."

The man and Eva exchange a look. It's quick, and I wouldn't have noticed if I wasn't watching them in that very moment. Are they concerned that I'm interested in Scarlett—romantically? The thought is absurd. And yet a tendril of warmth spreads through my body at the thought.

It's that thread that has been tugging at me since I arrived. It's the reason I wanted to help with the skate night. I'm thrown off by the idea, and yet I find joy in the prospect.

"Do you know what you want to get her?" Eva directs the question to Annabelle, but I don't miss the way she's looking at me.

Annabelle moves to the display case and frowns. "No. Do you know what she likes?"

Another glance at me from the baker herself. "Did you know... that Breckenridge has a secret?"

Annabelle's focus cuts to Eva. "Really? What kind of secret."

"Magic," Eva breathes.

And just like that, Annabelle is hooked. She moves closer to Eva and places her hands on the counter. "What kind of magic?"

"A long time ago, there was a magic well in this town. It was rumored that the water could grant wishes. It could save someone who was sick. It could heal the hurt." Her eyes flicker to mine briefly. "It could help two people fall in love."

Annabelle sighs. "Really?"

Eva grins down at her and leans onto the counter like she was when we arrived. "Really," she whispers. "But only if you are pure in heart."

"What happened to it?" Annabelle whispers back. A hush falls over the whole bakery, and even I don't dare move for fear of breaking the spell.

"It was destroyed a long time ago."

Annabelle's form slumps, and she frowns. "Oh."

Eva curls her finger toward Annabelle. "Can you keep a secret?"

Annabelle's interest flares to life again, and she nods. I watch the whole thing with awe. The people in this town have a knack for drawing people in. It isn't just Eva. Meredith and Holly have the same effect as well.

Eva leans forward, but I can still hear her soft words. "I believe the well still runs. My shop sits atop it. So, if you want to pick something special for Miss Scarlett to help her wishes come true, then I would suggest those sugar plum cookies for her, as well." Her eyes dart to meet mine, and a chill sweeps down my spine.

Annabelle jumps up and down with excitement. "Yes. Let's do that." She turns to me and grins. "Can we, Dad? Can we get Miss Scarlett the magic cookies?"

I shrug. "I don't see why not." It would be silly for me to admit that I believe in such things as magic, but it won't hurt to give Scarlett a boost for the dreams she already has in the works.

While Eva bags up the goodies, the man standing a few feet away takes a step toward me. "How are you enjoying our town?"

I stare at him in confusion.

Eva laughs. "Kasper, meet my husband. Mayor Nick Foster."

Mayor. I chuckle and extend my hand. "It's nice to meet you. And this place is great. It's the perfect getaway."

Nick shakes my hand. "That's an interesting accent you have. Where are you from?"

My muscles tighten, expecting Annabelle to give us away again, but all she says is, "Averna."

Nick's brows crease. "I've never heard of the place."

"It's a small country up by England and Spain."

"Ah. Well, I hope you enjoy your visit." He turns to his wife. "I'll see you at lunch."

She nods, then hands the treats over the counter to Annabelle. I pull out my wallet, and she waves a hand through the air. "These are on the house."

I pause, then smile. "Thank you. That's very kind." I'm still reeling from the generosity that Eva showed us when we arrive at the rink.

Annabelle darts forward the second she sees her teacher, a small red box in hand. She practically shoves it into Scarlett's arms. "We got you something." She leans forward, a hand to the side of her mouth. "It's magic," she whispers.

Scarlett shoots a baffled smile in my direction as Annabelle swipes the skates from the floor and hurries to her bench to put them on.

Shoving my hands in my pockets, I stroll past Scarlett. "Think of it as a peace offering." It's all I can say before I slip off to my place on the bleachers.

Chapter 9

SCARLETT

"He's adorable!"

"No," I groan, "he's utterly ridiculous."

"It's *cute*." Holly gushes to me before taking a sip of her coffee. "He wants to *help*."

I scowl at her while tearing another piece off my pastry. "He wants a project to make him feel better about myself."

Holly shoots me a sharp look. "When did you become so jaded? I seem to remember a Scarlett who would have adored this sort of thing."

"Oh, I don't know..." I drawl. "Could it be the fact that all my money for my business got stolen and the guy who did it hasn't been found yet?"

To her credit, my friend offers me a sympathetic frown. "Still nothing, huh?"

I shake my head. "But that's not why I wanted to get coffee

with you this morning. Kasper is getting on my last nerve. It's like everything he does hits that one spot—you know, the one that itches and you just can't reach it right?"

Holly snorts. "Are you sure that it's not something else?"

"*Meaning*?" I chew on my pastry, my gaze sharp enough to make her hesitate but not entirely shy away from what she's about to say.

"Meaning maybe you like him."

I huff but don't argue. I know what she's talking about. A small part of me—the exhausted part of me—wishes I could accept his help. It's the same part of me that loves reading romance novels and roots for the hero to win the heart of his maiden.

There's just one problem. Kasper may be a prince, but I can't be his sweetheart.

Holly nudges me from across the table, worry lining her face. "You know what you need?"

"What's that?" I murmur without emotion. I know what I need. I needed a better financial manager, and I need to find a way to save my rink in less than three weeks.

"A night out."

A combination of a snort and a huff bursts from me—a sound I never thought I could make. "You do realize that every day is precious for me. Every single moment I have needs to go toward trying to fix this problem. Holly, I'm drowning. I can't just go out—"

"The festival starts on Friday. The first night everyone is in the heart of the town. You and I both know people rarely visit the rink that night. You might as well keep the lights off and come out with Lucian and me." Holly reaches for my hand and squeezes my fingers with her own. "Clear your head. Maybe reconsider Kasper's offer."

I shoot her a glare. "I'm not a charity case—"

"I know that. I just... You need to make sure you're taking care of yourself, too. We're going to avoid everything downtown on opening night and head over to the Frosted Wonderland. They're doing a celebration there, too. Lucian says Ash is trying something new. There's going to be a sleigh ride and hot chocolate. It probably won't be all that busy. You might like it."

Maybe she's right. I've been running myself ragged. I have plans for another skate night on Saturday, but the flyers are already out, and several of the shops have donated again. But Friday? It would give me time to forget about the mess I'm in—give me distance to see if there's something I've missed.

Finally, I nod. "I'll be there."

Holly grins wider than I've seen in a long time. "Good. We'll meet you at the sleigh ride first thing—just in case more people attend than Ash is expecting. We don't want to have to wait in the cold for the next ride."

I nod numbly. Hopefully, I won't regret taking a night off.

The Frosted Wonderland's main focal point is a palace constructed of logs made from ice. Ash somehow figured out how to construct the bones of the place with large, frozen poles. Then he set up a water system that slowly poured over the structure to give it depth and added beauty. The ice logs don't look like logs anymore, but rather walls of ice that have shot from the earth itself.

The size alone would have been impressive, but it's the lights that make the place shine—literally. Multicolored lights flicker and glow from within the ice. In the dark, the whole place is a wonderland that rivals anything I've ever seen.

My breath comes out in white puffs, and I shift my weight from one foot to the next as I try to stay warm. I don't see Holly anywhere. We're supposed to be going on the sleigh ride.

A huge red sleigh that can seat at least four people—maybe five or six—is parked beneath some large evergreens. Four white horses are set to pull the contraption. It's genius to have an attraction like this one. No one else in town has anything like it, and it makes me wonder if I should look into special attractions myself.

"Sorry we're late!" Holly's breathing is ragged. "We got held up." She flashes me a smile, then nods to the sleigh. "Looks like we planned it right. It might just be the three of us." She glances over her shoulder, and I climb onto the sleigh.

When I sit down, I find that Holly is still staring behind her. "Where did he go?" She glances back at me apologetically. "Hold on. I think someone stopped him. Guess I'm going to have to track him down. *Again.*"

I stand to disembark when the sleigh shifts, and a familiar excited voice echoes through the trees around us. "Miss Scarlett! Why are you here?"

I don't even look down at Annabelle. My eyes are locked on Kasper as he grips the sides of the sleigh where he stands. His eyes bore into mine, and I can practically hear the last conversation we had ringing in my ears.

Think of it as a peace offering.

The cookies had been utterly divine. So wonderful, in fact, that I've been tempted to purchase some of my own. I would have, too, if it wasn't for Holly's insistence that I save every penny.

I offer him a small smile—my own peace offering. Then I glance down at the beautiful little girl standing before me. "Probably the same reason you are. I'm here to see what this Frosted Wonderland is all about." I crouch closer to her and whisper, "Is it as pretty as your palace?"

Annabelle beams at me. "It's even better."

Her answer brings a smile to my face. For all the bad that's happening in my life, Annabelle is a bright spot. I rise again, prepared to get off the sleigh ride so I don't have to be stuck seated beside her father, but the driver of the sleigh turns where he sits at the front. "We'll pulling out. Please be seated."

Kasper's expectant look has me taking an unsure step backward. Strange that it's enough to make me reconsider. My hands seek purchase on the sleigh bench, and I settle close to the far side of the sleigh.

Annabelle takes the seat across from me, facing me with a wide, bright smile. When her father moves to sit beside her, she shakes her head. "I want my own seat."

He hesitates.

"Please be seated," the driver repeats.

Kasper does as he's told, taking the spot beside me.

I glance at him, my body warming. The horses move forward, tugging the sleigh after them. Annabelle turns around almost immediately and faces forward, perched on her knees.

Holly is going to get a kick out of this when she hears what happened. It's the only thing I allow to cross my mind. My hands are clasped tightly in my lap. Unspoken words from our last conversation continue to hang between us. I know I should apologize for being short with him. I feel like I need to plead my case. But I don't do either. We ride down a trail away from the lights and music of the palace.

Trees in the wooded area are glowing, strung up to match the palace. It's quiet—peaceful. It'd be romantic if I let it.

"I hope you know..." Kasper murmurs so quietly only I can hear him, "I just wanted to help."

I nod, my throat tight. "I know."

"Annabelle adores you. It would be my pleasure to—"

I shake my head and force a smile. "I really appreciate the offer, I do. It's just..." My brows furrow, and I try to come up with the words to explain why I'm being so stubborn about this. "If you come and save my rink, then how do I know if I should keep it?" My face heats quickly, and I'm grateful it's dark enough he can't see my blush. "I need to do this—on my own. I have to prove to everyone else... and myself... that I can fix it—that I deserve it." I blow out a heavy breath and shut my eyes briefly. "I know that probably sounds silly—"

"I get it."

His words have my eyes flying to meet his, and I hold my breath.

Kasper shifts in his seat, but it doesn't appear he's capable of getting comfortable. "I may not agree with it... but I can understand where you're coming from."

Relief pools in my middle. "Really?"

He tilts his head and gazes at me with that unnerving stare of his. "There is value in knowing you're capable of doing something especially when it feels the world is against you or... that your path has already been set out for you." He's quiet for a moment.

I've never felt more vulnerable than I am in this moment. He sees me—truly sees me. My insides knot up without a prayer of being untangled any time soon. "Thank you," I say breathily.

"I still want to help," he murmurs.

Stiffening, I watch him reproachfully. He chuckles.

"Money isn't the only way I can do that, you know." He shifts again. The backs of his hands rest on his knees, and he looks down at them. "That skate night was a big hit. I hear you're planning more." He sweeps his gaze up to meet mine, and my heart loses all sense of control. "Let me help with that. Flyers. Getting out the word. Finding donors. Whatever you want, I'm at your disposal."

I blink several times. His offer is generous. More than generous, it's exactly the sort of thing I need right now. I swallow back the lump of emotion in my throat and nod. "I'd like that."

Chapter 10

KASPER

Despite Scarlett keeping most of her financial details a secret, I discover enough that I feel I can give her a plan to start off with. My parents made sure to educate me on more than simply running our country.

I learned how to make a budget and where to cut costs. I have a knack for seeing numbers and how to ease financial burdens in most cases. Just because I was raised with wealth doesn't mean I don't know how to manage it.

The words flow through my mind as I trudge along the snow-covered sidewalks toward the rink. Scarlett's plan to raise money is a good start, but making some cuts will make the money go further.

The rink is quiet when I arrive. Not even the lights over the ice are on. Most of the lighting comes from the windows high up on the walls. The whole place is bathed in a natural glow that makes it feel ethereal. While the entire town has been decked out in

Christmas decorations and twinkling lights, the rink seems almost empty.

I never noticed it before. Looking at this place with new eyes makes it painfully obvious that Scarlett is running it on the bare minimum.

Perhaps my plan to go through her paperwork and taxes won't do as much good as I thought.

Heaving a weary sigh, I move across the open area toward the counter where Scarlett rents the shoes out. A soft glow comes from a hallway to the side, and I follow it to find Scarlett seated behind a desk.

Her elbows are on the desk, and her head is in her hands. Her hair is pulled up into a messy bun—her preferred style. If she heard me enter, she doesn't show it. I fold my arms and lean against the open doorway.

My heart aches just watching her. It would be so much easier for her to accept my gift—my donation. But I know better than to point that out again. She'd shut me down harder than anyone has before.

I clear my throat, and her head snaps up. It's clear she's been crying. No tears streak her face, but her eyes are red.

Immediately, I push away from the doorway, itching to pull her into a hug. The desire to do so has me lurching to a halt.

Scarlett sniffles and offers me an embarrassed smile. "Sorry. I was just..." She looks down at the spread of documents. "The bank called."

I stiffen further, not wanting to prevent her from telling me any vital information that will help me with her situation.

"They're offering me a reprieve."

"That's—good, isn't it?" Why the tears? Why does it look as though she's about to crumble?

"Yes and no," she sighs. "Initially, they were preparing the paperwork to put the place up for a short sale toward the end of the month. After that first skate night... I guess they saw potential they didn't want to snuff out. They said if I can raise enough to pay what's past due by Christmas, they'd pull some strings."

I clench my hands at my sides to fight the instinct to pull out my checkbook again. She wants to do this on her own. I have to let her. "Okay, so what does that mean... for you? Can you raise that kind of money?" I don't know how much it costs to run this place. I'm assuming if she's late on the mortgage, she's likely late on other bills as well. Securing the building won't do any good if it doesn't have power.

She falls back in her chair and swings it from side to side. "I don't know. That first night was great. It gave me a good start on it. But it could have been a fluke. Tonight, we're in the midst of the festival. People tend to gravitate toward the food and fun in town. Then there's the Frosted Wonderland. The owner is trying to turn it into something more." She drags both hands down her face with a groan. "There's only so much money out there. People have to decide where to spend it for the holidays. I... I just don't think I'm a priority."

Gritting my teeth, I again fight the urge to tell her she needs to stop being so stubborn. I can help. It's all I feel I'm even good for at this point.

Her eyes grow distant, and I take a step closer.

"Have you considered telling people that you're trying to save this place? Perhaps people could donate—"

She scowls, and I have my answer. But that look won't stop me from trying to figure out a way to do just that. If I can hide my donations behind the citizens of this town, I'm going to do it. Scarlett sits up straighter. "The best way to bring in money right now is to have those raffles. It doesn't look like much, but it's what brought in the most last week."

"And you have a lot of options again?"

She frowns. "Not as much as I'd like."

I nod, but an idea starts forming in my mind. She needs some bigger ticket items, and I know exactly how to get them. She doesn't have to know they're not all donated. "I'll head out and see what else I can find."

Her eyes cut to meet mine, but she doesn't object. Good. I don't have the heart to fight her right now. All my energy is being used to keep myself from shoving the money down her throat.

❋ ❋ ❋

"How did you..." Scarlett's voice dies in her throat, cut off by emotion as she takes in the spread I procured.

I beam at her. After swearing the local businesses to secrecy, I paid for several services outright for tonight's event and the following week. "And I told each business to make sure and spread the word. We want as many people as possible coming, if only to purchase raffle tickets."

Her misty eyes lift to meet mine, mouth still hanging open. "I don't know what to say. How did you get them to agree..."

He shrugs. "I have talents you don't even know about."

Scarlett lunges for me, wrapping her arms around me in a tight hug. As quickly as it starts, it ends when she pulls away from me, not even giving me a chance to return the hug. She pushes her hands into her back pockets and rocks onto her heels, not meeting my eyes. "Thank you."

I'm still reeling from the feel of her body pressed against mine. It's been so long since I had any contact with a woman—but holding Scarlett does something to me. The feeling is small, like a whisper next to my ear. It sends a shiver of pleasure down my spine, and I have to force myself to focus on her when she speaks again.

"I don't know how you did it, but this is going to be great."

"That's not even the best part," I offer. At her surprised look, I chuckle. "I left some tickets at each establishment. People can purchase tickets even if they can't come to the skate night."

Her eyes widen considerably. "What?"

I shrug again, loving the light of hope I see in her eyes. "You said people don't usually make it out to the rink on festival nights. I take it that's why you were at the Frosted Wonderland last night. So… I figure we'll get them however we can. Some of them even agreed to have the raffles as part of their tables at the event tonight."

Scarlett gasps. "That's the best idea I've ever heard." She jumps up, and her hands cover her mouth. She pulls them away only to say, "That takes out the need for advertising."

I smile. There's no way I'm going to tell her that I also paid the local radio station to remind people of the event.

She hugs me once more, and this time, I let my hands come

around her waist. I breathe her in. Even if it's for a couple seconds, I let myself partake of this piece of heaven.

The rest of the morning and early afternoon, Scarlett is in much higher spirits. She's more animated, and I can't help but wonder if this is the woman she used to be—before she found herself in the throes of financial ruin. That thought alone gives me pause. There has to be something more—a bigger reason for her to shut down so easily around me.

Scarlett hasn't hidden the fact that she didn't trust me after learning about my royal pedigree. There's definitely something else.

Her eyes find mine as we continue to prepare for the event tonight, and her smile falters. She looks away, but my stare remains fixed on her. "What?" she whispers.

"I can't help but wonder about something."

She stiffens visibly. If I'm not mistaken, her hands tremble slightly. It's as if she realizes something isn't adding up for me. "Okay."

I tap my finger on the desk that sits between us. "You mentioned the bank was going to sell the place at the end of the year. But you've only just started having financial issues. Haven't you been open for—"

"I've run this place since I stopped competing professionally. Two years."

My brows lift, and a memory stirs. That's why she looks so familiar. She was a professional ice dancer. I push aside all the questions that start to flow freely in my mind. "Your financial struggles only just started happening."

She nods, not looking at me as she gathers a stack of papers and hits them against the hard surface of the desk. "That's right."

"How does one go from running a business successfully to suddenly having nothing?"

Scarlett flinches, and I regret the way I phrased my question. "I suppose it's not surprising that you started putting the pieces together."

I grow still.

"And I guess I owe you something... seeing as you're helping me so much." She sighs and glances at me once more. "I didn't just suddenly become bad with money. I was doing great. My financial advisor—well, he was my manager first—when I retired, he started managing everything I'd earned from skating." Her hands shake as the words continue to spill from her lips. "Turns out, he got tired of getting a paycheck and decided to drain everything I had."

I jump to my feet, fury building. "He *what*?"

She doesn't react, merely continues. "He took money from other people, too. But apparently, he's been missing for a few months. I made the mistake of not looking too closely at the statements coming in the mail and..." She lifts her hands and shoulders. "That's what I deserve I guess."

"You didn't *deserve* any of that," I seethe. My mind is whirling with this information. Her financial distress is completely out of her hands. How can she sit there and tell me she wants to fix it when she isn't at fault? I want to holler at her to be smarter, to accept my help in the way I want to give it. She's a victim, not a person with poor financial and business sense.

"Kasper," her voice is soft and calm. "It's fine."

"It most certainly is not," I growl. "And you're telling me that they can't find him? That he just poofed into nothingness?"

She shrugs. "That's the last update I got."

"What about insurance? What about—"

Her blush deepens, and she squeezes her eyes tight. "The problem is he was managing my accounts separate from the company he'd started working for. They don't have any obligation to me. I was a fool for not vetting any of it."

"And that's why you think you deserve this?" My chest is heaving. I can't explain why this is tearing me apart as much as it is. Perhaps it's because the genuine and good woman before me is carrying everything on her shoulders without allowing others to come to her aid. It's backward in every sense of the word.

"Will you just *sit down*? I've already been through everything you're feeling. There's nothing I can do now except try to save this place and move forward." She gives me a look that warns me not to offer my money again.

And I die a little bit inside when I heed that request.

Chapter 11

SCARLETT

I'll be the first to admit that Kasper's concern is sweet. I saw it in the way his jaw tightened last night when I told him more than I planned. I saw it in his eyes, too. There was hatred in that gaze—not for me, but for my manager.

Unfortunately, I don't have the energy to vent about it anymore. There's nothing I can do to change that I've lost the money. All I can do is try to save up enough to get a second chance.

Right now, I have another looming issue.

I groan as I lean back in my office chair. My focus today hasn't been up to par. I can't seem to get through the paperwork I have for the upcoming skate night. All I can think about is Kasper and those eyes that desperately wanted to help.

Heat blooms in my chest, and a smile reaches across my face. The man is a literal prince, and I'm absolutely crushing on him.

It's a ridiculous notion.

More than ridiculous, it's impossible.

He's a prince.

I'm drowning in debt.

He's not even an American citizen!

I can't allow myself to get distracted by someone like him—especially not right now. I need every braincell working on my own problems—problems I've been so stubborn about fixing myself.

Lately, this little worm of doubt has been creeping into my determination to be my own fixer. Am I wrong in refusing help? It would be so easy to accept that check Kasper is prepared to write.

A sigh bursts from my chest, and I shake my head as I spin my chair from side to side. I know I'm right to refuse it. Nothing in life worth having is free. Eventually, I know I would regret accepting such a generous gift.

Kasper is sweet and generous. He didn't even wait for me to ask for help before making his offer. But he won't be sticking around, and that's what I'll continue to remind myself of. This crush of mine is merely an infatuation brought on by him being so helpful.

His face flashes in my mind. That smile. His eyes. Everything about him draws me in and makes me want to trust him.

I'm facing a framed picture of myself at one of my last Olympic events when there's a knock on my office door.

I swing my chair around, expecting to see Holly, but it's not her.

Sucking in a sharp breath as warmth spreads across my cheeks,

I slowly rise from my chair. "Kasper? What are you doing here? I don't have a lesson scheduled with Annabelle today..." My voice trails off as I take him in.

He's wearing that long, black wool coat as he always does. He's got a red scarf draped around his neck, and he's leaning in the doorway as casually as if he owns the place.

My heart ticks up at the sight of him, reminding me that while crushes may be ridiculous, they're still very much real. I clasp my hands in front of myself, waiting for his response, not missing the way his own focus sweeps across my form.

Kasper's eyes finally land on mine, and his soft smile makes my legs go numb. If I weren't so down on my luck, I might have listened to Holly and allowed myself to have some fun. Back when I traveled the world with my skating, I didn't have time for relationships. But flings? Fun dates with strangers I never planned to see again? Those I used to get behind.

I shake off the memories, realizing I missed what he asked. "I beg your pardon?"

Kasper arches a brow. "I promise it's not a date."

The searing heat in my cheeks intensifies. Shoot. What did he say?

He pushes away from the door and moves farther into my office. "Brunch. It's a little late for breakfast, so I thought you might like to get something to eat." Kasper motions to my dismal office. The only natural light comes from two small rectangular windows too high to see out of. "I think you should get out of the office and get some sunshine. The skate night is coming up, and you're going to be spending far too much time here as it is."

A wry smile tugs at my lips. "And you think I should spend that time with you?" I can't help the teasing tone that slips between the words. I can't tell if he notices the shift in my voice. If he does, he doesn't show it.

"Annabelle is making a gingerbread house with Meredith and Holly."

This time I lift a brow. If Holly is helping Meredith with Annabelle, then she's more than likely the reason Kasper has shown up to whisk me away from my work. "Is that so?"

Kasper chuckles. "Before you ask—"

"Holly put you up to this, didn't she?"

He shrugs. "All I'm going to say is that she made several good points. Sometimes we need breaks. And you've been working too hard."

"That sounds an awfully lot like what Holly might say."

"Have I mentioned how much I like her?" Kasper stops in front of my desk and places his palms on the smooth wooden surface. He grins like he knows I won't turn him down. How can I? When my best friend and my crush gang up on me, I don't have a chance.

"I suppose I'm outnumbered."

His voice takes on a low, husky quality. "I suppose you are."

Goosebumps attack, and I can't think of a single reason I should turn him down. "Okay," I concede, "and it's not a date."

He doesn't react immediately, but then he shakes his head slowly. Side to side, his eyes not leaving mine. "Not unless you want it to be."

I turn away from him before he can catch sight of the blush that threatens to give me away yet again. My coat hangs on a rack to my left, and I snatch it before taking my time to push my arms into the sleeves. "You have any ideas of where you'd like to go?" I ask, not looking at him over my shoulder.

"There's this place in town across from City Hall called—"

I turn. "Sage and Salt." I've only been to the restaurant a handful of times in the last two years. It's not a five-star experience by any means, but it's as close as Breckenridge will come to one. Folks out here definitely pick the place for romantic evenings.

But it's not evening now.

And this isn't a date.

Kasper nods. "Is it any good?"

I nod.

"Great. I hope you're hungry."

Before I can restrain myself, I murmur, "Famished."

※ ❄ ※

KASPER PICKS UP HIS FORK AND TAKES ANOTHER BITE OF the omelet drizzled with truffle sauce. "It's not all it's cracked up to be, you know. Nothing like the stories you might read in popular romance novels."

I grin. "Are you sure? Because from where I'm sitting, being a prince seems like it's pretty great."

He smirks right back at me. "Okay, let's put it this way. I told you I'm the second of three. My eldest brother is going to be king. My youngest is the favorite. So where do you suppose that leaves me?"

I shrug and take a bite out of my gourmet burger. It's not quite a brunchy sort of meal, but I warned Kasper I was starving.

"I'll tell you where." Kasper eyes my burger with amusement. "My responsibilities are almost nonexistent if you compare them to what my brothers have to do. I was raised to marry well and start a family. I show up at functions and charities. I put on a smile, wave, and let the country gawk at the man who lost his wife too soon."

My heart lurches, and the amusement fades from my soul. Before me sits a prince who simply wants to be a man—someone who can live his life in peace away from the spotlight. It resonates with me and my own past. I lived in the spotlight too, and there was nothing so freeing as buying my rink and starting my business.

He must read the sadness in my eyes, because he offers me a small, reassuring smile. "It got to the point where I hated being put on stage like that. I don't want Annabelle to have to suffer through that life, either." Kasper glances around the moderately busy restaurant, and a serene expression replaces the distant one. "I really like this town. Breckenridge isn't like other places I've visited."

"Yeah, I know what you mean," I whisper, also glancing through the restaurant. "It's one of the reasons I moved here."

Kasper swings his focus to me. "Great minds think alike."

The way he says it makes me wonder if he's considering doing something similar. But that would be crazy, right? Kasper is royalty. He has duties to uphold. I've heard of other members of various royal families walking away from their responsibilities. But would Kasper actually consider it?

I don't dare ask. I refuse to give him any reason to believe I may like him more than I should.

Dropping my gaze to my fries, I pick one from the pile and nibble on it. "How does Annabelle like it here?"

"She loves it."

His voice is so quiet that I can't help but look up at him. He's watching me with that look again—the one that's capable of making a crowd of women swoon. I smile, nodding again. "Good."

Good? Seriously? That's all I can come up with?

I clear my throat and fight the blush that's threatening to burst once more from my chest and my face. "So besides feeling like you're a puppet on a stage, is there anything good about being a prince?"

He seems to consider my question. Then his lips curl into a devilish smile. "Since I'm not the future king, I have more freedom to do as I wish—if only a little."

"Yeah? And what do you do with that freedom?"

Kasper doesn't respond right away, though his eyes never leave mine. Finally, he murmurs, "Take spontaneous trips to little towns in Idaho... and spend time with pretty ice skaters."

I snort. Then I cover my mouth, and my face fills with that annoying heat. I can't meet his gaze anymore. This is the furthest he's gone in his flirtations. There's no way to deny it. I reach for my drink, frantically needing something to take my mind off his words, but in the process, I knock the glass over.

Water slooshes across the table, and we both reach for the glass. His fingers brush mine, and I yank my hand away. "Sorry," I mutter, yanking my napkin from my lap, grateful the water was mostly gone anyway.

When I risk another look in his direction, I find him watching me, amusement dancing in his eyes. "Don't worry about it." He rights the glass and waves over a waitress for more napkins.

Holly's going to get an earful when I get my hands on her. I fully intend on blaming her for all of this.

Chapter 12

KASPER

I pick up my phone and stare at the caller's name.
James.
Again.

I don't want to talk to him. He's the only one who attempted to prevent me from leaving the country. I know before I answer that he's going to tell me to come back home—mostly because I've received messages confirming as much.

Depositing the phone back on my bed, I glance over to Annabelle, who is completely enthralled with a children's Christmas special playing on the television. Her eyes sparkle much like her mother's did during the holiday season.

No one will ever be able to convince me it wasn't a good idea to come out to this small town. Both of us have benefited from the anonymity. Soon enough, we will both be heading back to our home.

Away from the snow.

Away from magic.

Away from Scarlett.

A knot of desperation forms in my chest. I've only been in this tiny town for a few weeks, and already I know I'm attached to her in ways I shouldn't be. James will throw a fit if he learns I have feelings for someone new.

Not just anyone—an American woman.

After losing Rose, I told myself I would never marry again. I'm more than capable of raising our daughter on my own. And she has the influence of our extended family for anything I may not be good at.

Then I met Scarlett.

Annabelle must feel my gaze on her. She turns to look at me, then cocks her head and grins. "What?" she chirps.

I look into those innocent eyes, and I know that I'm wrong. Deep down, I know she deserves to have someone in her life. She doesn't remember her mother. Eventually, she's going to need one.

Annabelle gets to her feet, her brows creasing together and a small frown forming on her lips. "Are you sad?"

I still, realizing the expression on my face most definitely gives me away. "I'm not *sad*," I insist, crouching down in front of her. "Just thinking."

"About what?" She reaches for my hand. "Do you miss grandma?" The way she tilts her head, that concern, it rips at my heart. I've taken her from her family for this trip, and while I know she's enjoyed it, that doesn't mean she hasn't felt a little lonely.

"Maybe a bit. Do *you* miss grandma?" I settle down in front of her, taking a seat on the floor.

She nods.

"Do you want to go home early?"

Her face scrunches briefly, and she tilts her head, considering. "Not yet."

I can't fight the smile that tugs at my lips. She saves me the need to ask her what it is that makes her want to stay as she climbs into my lap and snuggles close.

"If we go, then I'm going to miss Holly. And Miss Meredith. And Miss Scarlett." Her eyes meet mine once more, concern emanating from them. "I think they'll miss me, too."

I smile broadly. "I think you're right. They would miss you."

"Do you think we can come back? After we go home and see grandma and grandpa?"

That's a question I've been asking myself lately. I can't say for certain if we'll get the chance to visit, and that thought alone is enough to tear at my heart. Scarlett's face fills my mind, triggering a surge of desire. The more time I spend with the woman, the more addicted I become. I practically crave it. Her stubborn insistence that she take care of herself infuriates me, and yet I can't help but admire her for it.

"Daddy?"

I jump and stare down at Annabelle, noting the concern in her eyes. A chuckle escapes my throat. "I don't see why not. It'd be nice to come to visit as much as we can, don't you think?"

She smiles, and her eyes brighten. "Really?"

I nod. "Maybe we should look for a place to call our own. What do you think?"

All at once, her brows knit together. "But then we wouldn't be able to visit Meredith and Holly."

I laugh again, pulling her into a tight hug and placing a kiss to her brow. "I'm sure we could manage a few visits." My heart tightens with anticipation and excitement at the thought of finding a place here—one we can visit whenever we want, even if it's for a weekend here or there. That will be enough.

My phone buzzes across the room again, this time more insistently than before. Someone's calling. It's probably James. Again. I heave a sigh, but I refuse to let him lecture me about how long I'm staying. If something really pressing is going on back home, my father would call. Or Alexander. They're the leaders of our country and the only ones who'd be able to convince me to cut this trip short.

"Are you ready to go to your skating lesson?"

Annabell nods, climbing out of my lap. "I drew a picture for Miss Scarlett."

"I'm sure she'll love it," I say before she hands it to me. Then my heart stops. I can't breathe. In the picture is a little girl holding hands with two individuals. On one side is a woman who can only be Scarlett, and on the other is me. Annabelle has drawn a heart around the three of us. Beneath the heart is the word "*luv.*" Annabelle is young, but she's been working on her sounds. Most of her pictures have at least one word scrawled across the bottom of the page—usually spelled wrong. I hate that I'm not sure Scarlett should see it. What will she think when she reads that word?

"What's the matter?" Annabelle asks. "Did I spell it wrong?" She peers over the edge of the paper and frowns. "I always spell stuff wrong."

"It's fine, kiddo." My tongue burns with the desire to ask her why she chose this word for her drawing, but I leave it alone. Annabelle is still young. It's probably just a word she likes. "I'm sure she's going to love it," I repeat. "You're getting really good at drawing people, and this one is my favorite."

Her bright eyes find mine. "Really?"

I nod. "Now, get your boots. We don't want to be late."

❄ ❄ ❄

IN THE BEGINNING, I WATCHED MY DAUGHTER SKATE, loving the way she took to the ice. But now, I can't seem to drag my eyes from the ice queen who has captured my heart. If things were different, I would ask her out without a second thought.

The more I think about it, the more I can't help asking myself why I can't do that very thing.

Because she'll probably turn me down.

Scarlett has so much going on right now. She doesn't have time to deal with a new relationship. Besides, I'm the last person she'd want in her life. I'm a foreigner. I'm part of a royal family. There are certain types of scrutiny I'm sure she'd rather avoid.

And yet I can't help the way my mind drifts to that possibility. I don't plan on leaving for a couple weeks. What's the harm in asking her out? As long as she's interested, that is.

She catches my eye and immediately looks away. It's clear she noticed my staring. Does it bother her? From this distance, I can't tell. A smile tugs at my lips. I'm going to find out.

After the lesson, Annabelle insists she needs to use the restroom, and I get my chance.

Scarlett sits on a bench that's pushed up against a cinder brick wall. She hunches over her skates, unlacing them with swift movements, and I move closer.

Resting my forearm against the wall, I glance down at her.

She stills her movements, and her eyes drift upward. I'm probably crazy for even considering what I'm going to say, but the words spill out of my mouth before I have a chance to reconsider.

"Go out with me."

Scarlett blinks, straightening further. "I beg your pardon?"

A wry smile pulls at the corner of my mouth. "Let me take you on a date. A real one."

Her lips purse, and her focus shifts toward the bathrooms before she tugs one of her skates from her feet. "I don't think that's a good idea."

"Why not?"

She removes the other skate and places it beside her. "You know why."

"Do I?"

"Kasper," she whispers, getting to her feet so we're closer to eye-level. "You've been wonderful—"

I move closer to her, pushing off the wall as I do. To my delight, she doesn't back away. "You're working too hard. You deserve a break."

"And I've gotten them," she murmurs.

I shake my head. "When was the last time you let someone take care of you?"

Her brows pull together, and the nervous smile that forms on her lips draws my attention. "With all due respect," she hedges, "you're a client."

"My daughter is your client."

She rolls her eyes. "There's no difference, Kasper."

I love the way she says my name. It briefly distracts me from the fact that she's trying to brush off my advances. Even I can hear the hesitation in her decision to do so.

"I won't be here much longer. We should take advantage of that fact."

"That's another reason we shouldn't... what if we..."

I move closer. This time, we're inches apart. She lifts her chin to maintain her gaze, and I lower my voice so there's no chance anyone will hear us—specifically my daughter. "It's just a date. And if it were to become more..." I shrug, leaving my statement hanging. If I'm honest with myself and her, I'd tell her that nothing would make me happier than to see where a relationship with her could go. But I'm not brazen enough to say that.

Her closeness, the way her eyes spark with curiosity, and the sharp intake of breath—all of it spurs me closer. I've only known her for a couple weeks, and I shouldn't be this drawn to her, but I am. I'm willing to admit it. I don't want to lose the small opportunity I may have to investigate these feelings further.

I take her chin in my grasp, holding her in place. My gaze sweeps over her features, and the temptation to kiss her beats my reservations into obscurity.

Then the squeak of a door opening tears us apart.

Scarlett stumbles back a step, her chest rising with effort. She brings her hands to her hair as she turns to see Annabelle skipping toward us. My daughter is oblivious to the tension between us as she moves to our pile of belongings.

"I drew a picture for you," she announces.

My eyes never leave Scarlett. She swallows hard, her cheeks

flushed as her gaze shifts to Annabelle. "Really?" The murmured question comes out as more of a squeak than anything else. "Let me see it?"

I watch her closely, waiting for the reaction I know is surely to come. Maybe it's reaching to believe that she's as interested in me as I am in her. But I can't completely disregard the attraction I feel from her. She smiles at Annabelle as she takes the paper from her outstretched hands. Then she unfolds the picture and grows still.

Her eyes flick up to meet mine, and fresh color sweeps across her cheeks.

Annabelle stands on her toes and peers at the picture. "Do you like it?"

Scarlett starts at Annabelle's question. She drags her attention to my daughter, and her smile returns. "It's beautiful. Are we ice skating?"

Annabelle nods, pointing. "But my dad doesn't know how to skate so he's wearing shoes."

Her eyes shift to meet mine once more. "I suppose we'll have to change that."

My daughter, bless her heart, nods. "You should teach him. I get to watch *Frozen* with Holly tomorrow. You could teach my dad then."

Scarlett bites back a smile. We both do. "I think I could manage that."

Chapter 13

SCARLETT

"What am I *doing*?" I cover my face with my hands and let out a strangled laugh. "I practically asked him out."

"How so?" Holly takes a sip of her coffee, but the smirk that tugs at her lips is all the evidence I need to believe I've done something she wholeheartedly approves of.

My hands fall from my face, and I give her a look. "You know exactly what I mean."

"What? That you told that sweet little girl you'd teach her father how to skate? One on one? Without her?" Holly snickers. "I knew you couldn't hold out. That man is..." She sighs. "He's perfect for you, Scarlett."

"He's leaving in less than two weeks," I mutter with exasperation. "I don't know why I'm even bothering."

"Because he's hot."

"That's not a good reason."

"Why not?" Holly presses. "If anyone deserves to be swept off their feet even for a night, it's you. Call this your Cinderella moment. He's literally a prince. And the day he's supposed to go back to his country is midnight. Enjoy yourself for once."

The more reasons she gives me to give in, the harder it becomes to make excuses. I can't exactly say I'm not ready for something serious, because this fling has no chance of becoming one.

"What if I get attached?" It's the only concern I can't seem to shake. I haven't been able to admit to my best friend how much I look forward to seeing him. I can't even admit that there are times during the day when I wish I could text him so we can hang out. Kasper is the only guy who has managed to make me smile in a long time.

When Holly doesn't respond, I force myself to look at her. Her eyes say it all. "You like him, don't you?"

I groan.

"I knew it!" Her howl of delight makes me duck my head. Several eyes shift to our table in the coffee shop.

"Shh!"

Her wicked grin spreads further across her face. "It's too late, isn't it? You already have a crush on him. That's why you're so scared."

"I'm not scared," I insist. "I'm just..." I groan for what feels like the hundredth time and shove my hands into my mussed hair. "There's so much going on. My life is in shambles, and in a few weeks, I don't even know where I'm going to live."

Holly frowns. "Please, let me help—"

My sharp look is enough to kill the request before she can finish it.

She looks away, and guilt slices through me with a vengeance. I still can't allow her to step in and clean up my mess.

I tighten my grip around the steaming coffee cup in my hands and stare at it hard. "Sorry."

"You don't have to be sorry, sweetie. This isn't your fault."

But it is. I've admitted to that time and again, yet Holly fails to see it.

"Let's get back to the issue at hand," she insists. "Kasper."

I shake my head, fighting the urge to laugh.

Holly leans forward, her voice low. "Don't think too hard about it. Have some fun. Whatever happens, happens. Seriously, take it from me. Sometimes you just have to give in and let fate decide."

My brows crease. Holly had been a tourist once. She ultimately decided to stay. But at least she's a U.S. citizen.

"I can see those cogs whirring, Scarlett. We both know what you're going to decide anyway." Holly shrugs. "Besides, if this whole thing with your rink doesn't work out… and the thing with Kasper does…" She laughs. "Then would it be so bad if you find a new path?"

My stomach flips. Can I trade one dream for something different?

❋ ❅ ❋

"You think you're ready for this?" I arch a brow, a pair of skates in my hands.

Kasper chuckles. The sound is soft, warm, and it wraps around me like a delectable caramel. He takes the skates from my hands, and his fingers brush against mine. "I'm sure I can handle it if Annabelle can."

I bite down on my lips, pressing them into a thin line to fight the grin that threatens to escape. There are people who are simply naturals when it comes to ice-skating, and there are others who… aren't.

My skates are already on, and I pop a hip as I watch him work to lace his skates. They're not tight enough, so I move to his side. "Here, let me."

His hands pause, and I kneel in front of him. "You want them to be snug—not too tight that they're painful, but secure enough that you don't break an ankle. They need to be an extension of your feet." I glance up at him, finding him watching me intently, and my heart stutters.

The moment we shared yesterday floods my mind, and I can't stop the flush from spreading across my cheeks. Despite the cool temperatures of the rink, I'm burning up.

I clear my throat as I move to the next skate. When I'm done, I move to get up, but he holds out a hand to help. I stare at the offering, wondering if taking it will only solidify what's growing between us.

Channeling Holly, I take his hand, and he pulls me to my feet. We're close, only our hands between us. Kasper stares down at me, his eyes searching for something. I can't breathe. This is the exact same situation as yesterday, and I know he's going to kiss me. I'm not sure I'm ready for that yet.

He lifts a free hand and brushes a strand of hair from my face. A chill skitters through my body, not entirely unpleasant. When I'm with him, I can forget my life is in shambles. I can let all my fears for the future fall away.

It's—freeing.

Exhaling, I shut my eyes to gather my faculties. I'm not going to allow myself to fawn over this guy. I'm not even sure this constitutes a first date. When I take a step back and open my eyes, I'm not prepared for the way his free hand darts out and wraps around my wrist. He's still got my other hand in his. I wait for him to say something—do something to indicate his intentions. Then he flashes me a smile as he brushes his thumbs in circles on the backs of my hands. "You might need to hold my hand… in case I fall."

I let out a surprised laugh. "Is that so? I doubt I'd be much help if you trip. We might both end up falling together."

He cocks his head, and that smile…

Goodness, that smile is enough to put me over the edge.

"Would that be so bad?" he purrs.

I blush again and shake my head, understanding exactly what he's getting at. Without his daughter present, he's definitely more forward. "You're being ridiculous." When I attempt to pull away, his grasp on my hand tightens. He brings it to his lips and brushes the softest kiss to my knuckles. Then he releases me.

I nearly stumble backward.

Trouble with a capital T. That's what this is.

What's more added on to the trouble I'm already in?

I toss him a flirtatious grin—as flirtatious as I can muster—over my shoulder before I head for the ice. The second my blades hit the cold surface, I'm free. I glide out and around the freshly frozen rink like I was born to live on it. Arching around in a wide circle, I pick up my pace. My blades chop at the ice with each step, and I hoist myself into the air for a triple before landing and gliding to stop.

My breaths are heavy, but the pent-up energy has been released.

"Show off," Kasper calls out from the entrance to the rink.

I spin around to face him, laugher bubbling up from my chest. "Well? Are you coming? Or not?"

He's holding onto the edges of the opening with a tight grip as he places one unsure skate on the ice. I bite back a smile and move toward him, slowly, gracefully. His head lifts to stare at me, a sheepish grin touching his lips. "Annabelle really does make this look easier than I thought."

"And you've really never skated before?"

Kasper chuckles. "Does it count if I was under ten?"

"No, I suppose not," I laugh, holding out my hand. "Okay, first you need to try not being so tense. You're going to fall. It's practically a rite of passage."

"Gee, that makes this so much more exciting."

I take hold of both of his now-gloved hands. "It's not as bad as you think." As I tug him backward, he glances at the ground. "Don't look at your feet. Look at me."

He lifts his eyes to meet mine, and once again, my pulse flutters. It's like a caged insect beating its wings wildly, trying to escape the glass jar it's been trapped in.

"There, see? One foot, then the other. Focus on your balance. It's like I said before. You need to make those skates part of you."

We spend the next thirty minutes on the basics. All the tips and tricks I can think of, I give him. He stays close to me. Toward the end of our session, he's more sure-footed—not a natural, by any means—but he's got more confidence.

"You were a professional skater, if I recall correctly," Kasper murmurs while we skate the perimeter of the rink.

I glance at him and nod.

"What made you give it up?"

I shrug. "A lot of things, I suppose. I was getting older. I wanted to settle down." I smile wistfully. "I wanted to open my own rink." A sigh bursts from my lips. "I got injured and competing just wasn't a possibility."

His eyes are on me, penetrating any walls I may fling up around me. I know what he wants to say. It's the same thing that Holly has said a thousand times before. He wants to help. I can't let him bring it up.

"Did you know there used to be a magic well here?"

A smile crosses his features. "I've heard, yes."

I sigh, rolling my shoulders. "Back when I opened this place, I thought it was a fun story. I figured that if a town like this could have a little bit of magic, then perhaps it was the perfect place to open a rink. I was drawn to this place. It's ridiculous, clearly, but—"

"I don't think it's ridiculous."

My gaze snaps to him, and I snort. "You're telling me you believe in such nonsense?"

He shrugs. "Why not? There are crazier things than a magic wishing well. The stories have to come from somewhere, right?"

We stop in the middle of the rink, staring at each other. I can see it in his eyes. He actually believes in magic. A laugh escapes me. "Of course you believe in that stuff. You're a prince. You're literally what fairytales are made of." My flippant statement dies in my throat when Kasper takes my hands in his and tugs me closer.

I stare down at where he's touching me, and a distinct sort of desire builds in my stomach. I may not believe in fairytales, but I can use that sort of magic right now.

With the rink?

With the man in front of me?

He drops one of my hands and reaches for me. His hand slides around the back of my neck, tilting my face so my eyes meet his. We're closer now. I can feel the warmth of his breath as it fans my face.

Kasper's brown eyes delve into mine, capturing me relentlessly.

Then he kisses me.

Chapter 14

KASPER

Scarlett tastes like sugar and cinnamon. She's delicious and intoxicating, and I already know this kiss won't be nearly enough to satisfy my craving for her. I pull her tighter against my chest, no longer caring about the impropriety of such an action.

I've been thinking about her since we shared that moment yesterday. She was in my dreams last night. She's been the object of every thought that entered my head since I woke up this morning.

Heat floods my body, and I'm impervious to the cold that surrounds us. Everything else falls away. It's just the two of us in existence at this moment. Though I've barely met this woman, I feel like I've known her for a lifetime.

I know her desires.

I know her wishes.

I know what makes her tick, the strength that overcomes anything thrown at her.

There's no question that I can see a future with her.

My family will think I've gone off the deep end, but I don't care. I can't shake the feeling that I need to protect this woman. This is why I came to Breckenridge.

There's nothing keeping me back home—not really. Other princes have abdicated their responsibilities in the past. My hand tightens around her waist, and our kiss deepens as I consider what my life—the life I have with my daughter—could look like with Scarlett at our sides.

It'd be just like Annabelle's picture.

Love.

I can't scare her off. While she may be moaning beneath my touch, leaning into me with her own soft caresses, I know I have to rein in these desires. It wouldn't do either of us any good if I push her too far.

Our chemistry aside, I know I could be happy with her. I need to tread carefully. This is more than having feelings for her. This is about finding someone I can see caring for Annabelle like her own mother would have.

Scarlett pulls back first. Her breaths are shallow, and her eyes are still closed.

I pull her whole body against me, pressing my hands to her back and allowing her to tuck her face into the crook of my neck. I've never felt this connected to a person. It's almost unreal the feelings that are surging through me.

If I weren't a more level-headed man, I could see myself calling up my family today to tell them I have no intention of coming home.

That would be insane.

Right?

I close my eyes tight and push aside the haze of desire that won't abate. The woman in my arms isn't mine. Not right now, but she could be one day—and that's something I fully intend to make happen.

When we part again, she tosses me an embarrassed smile and pushes off me so she's skating backward. "I think that ends our skating lesson."

I move toward her, not quite as awkwardly as a half hour ago. "Will I get another one?"

Scarlett tilts her head, her hands behind her back. "It's gonna cost you."

I smile wickedly. There are so many ways I could pay her back for lessons. And so many of those ideas would infuriate her. I continue moving after her, but I have no chance at catching her. She's too swift on her feet. "That works for me. I've got my checkbook—"

Her flirtatious smile falters, and she skids to a stop. "Kasper." Scarlett's tone holds a note of warning, and I laugh. As much as I would love to force her to take a check with whatever amount I deem appropriate, I know she won't accept it.

"Okay, I'll bite. What will it cost me?"

There's fresh caution in those eyes of hers, but a smile hovers just beneath the surface. She pulls her lower lip between her teeth, and I can see in real time her walls crumbling once again. "How about dinner?"

"Deal."

"This house has been on the market for two months."

"And why is that?" I ask the realtor. The house can hardly be called even that. It's a cottage at best. There are only two bedrooms and two bathrooms. But it sits on a good deal of land, surrounded by a forest of evergreens. It would take some time and money, but I can already see the potential.

My realtor taps a red fingernail on her matching lips and shifts the clipboard she has in her hand. "Honestly? It's overpriced. I don't think the sellers have figured out that people don't want land. They want something more move-in-ready. Those who want to move to Breckenridge plan to stay for the long haul. This cute place was built with vacationers in mind."

I nod. Her explanation makes sense. "Do you think they'd consider a lower offer?"

"It doesn't hurt to try. You said you plan on paying cash?"

I nod. "That's the plan."

Her lips thin when her smile widens. She's wearing far too much makeup, and her hair looks as though it's been teased until it begged for mercy. Thankfully, she appears to know her stuff. "Well, I have one more property I'd like to show you. Are you ready for the last one?"

Before I can answer, my phone vibrates and I pull it out.

I already know who's calling. James has been especially vague in all his messages in regards to the reasons he wants me home.

Even the handful of times I answered the call, he's only ever asked me to cut the trip short. No reasons. Nothing concrete.

Heaving a sigh, I hold up a finger to my realtor and walk away.

"Let me guess," I mutter into the phone as it reaches my ear, "you want me to come home."

"Yesterday," James snaps.

My brows lift. "You sound like you're in a mood."

He mutters an expletive, and I fight a grin. "You've been gone for two and a half weeks—nearly three. When you told mom that you were going on holiday, she was led to believe that you would be back within a fortnight. How much longer do you plan on staying in America?"

I glance at the cottage, already envisioning sharing it with Annabelle—and eventually Scarlett. James will flip a lid when he finds out about my plans, and I know better than to tell him I don't plan on coming back for good. "My plane tickets are scheduled for the day after Christmas."

James curses again. "The day after Christmas? Are you crazy?"

My humor flees a little faster. It's the first time I wonder just how wrong everything is back home. "Why do you want me back so bad?" I ask quietly.

"You're needed."

I snort.

"I mean it, Kas." His voice is quieter this time. He sounds utterly exhausted. "We need you home."

"Why?"

The silence on the other end stretches longer than I anticipate, and my pulse picks up. Something is definitely wrong. My ignoring my little brother has worn him down. All he needs is for me tip the scales a bit more. "Give me one good reason."

"Is this because of a girl?"

His question is like a punch to the gut. The air escapes my lungs. How does he know? "Are you having me tailed?"

"It *is* a girl!" James mutters another curse, and I can envision him pacing down the great hall in our parents' home. "Geez, Kasper. You're a bigger idiot than I thought."

"You're not doing yourself any favors in getting me to come home early. Annabelle and I are enjoying our vacation—a vacation we've more than needed since Rose passed."

"Don't bring Rose into this. She's been gone nearly four years."

"And the anniversary of her death is right around the corner."

"Your trip might have started off being a trip to get away from the memories, but it's not anymore. And if you think you can up and fall for some commoner—"

"You don't know what you're talking about," I interrupt him. "What I do in my spare time is none of your business."

"You're right. It's not. But whoever she is, she can't be important enough for you to stay when we need you back home. You have responsibilities!"

"Liar. I'm a glorified middle child in a royal family. My biggest responsibilities revolve around tiny shovels and giant scissors—something you are more than capable of handling."

James sighs, but it shifts into a groan. "Just... come home, Kas. I know you want more, but I can't give that to you. Not yet."

My laugh is void of humor. "Goodbye, James. I'll see you after Christmas and not a day sooner."

Scarlett's laugh blends with Annabelle's when we're skating around the rink. It's full tonight at the Ice Castle rink. My eyes lock with Scarlett's. A pretty flush spreads across her cheeks, and she looks away. It's only been a few days since our first kiss, yet it feels longer.

I can steal glances from her for the rest of my life and be perfectly happy to do so. The way she is with Annabelle makes me happier than I thought I could be after losing Rose. Scarlett has entered my heart, and I don't want to lose her.

Annabelle slows and turns her head over her shoulder to look back at me. "Hold my hand, Daddy."

Scarlett meets my gaze again, her smile intoxicating.

I skate forward and nearly fall flat on my face, much to Annabelle's delight. She giggles and looks up to Scarlett. "I think he needs more practice."

"I think you're right," Scarlett chuckles.

"Maybe we're going to stick around longer than we planned."

The woman I'm falling for stares at me with surprise. "Really?"

"I mean, we're going to have to head home to settle a few things, but I fully intend on coming back."

Annabelle gasps, her bright eyes turning to Scarlett. "That means I can keep taking lessons."

Scarlett's eyes don't leave mine. "You want to... stay?"

"If that's not going to mess with any of your plans."

She shakes her head quickly. "Of course not. I just didn't

think that you were able to do that... with your other responsibilities."

If only she knew how little I'm needed back home. I draw closer to her and brush the back of my hand against her cheek. This is the most intimate I've been with her in public, and we're both fully aware of it based on the way her eyes dart around the rink before landing on mine once more. I drop my hand and take her free one, forcing our trio to form a circle. "I'm thinking about buying some property here. Some land? Maybe a little house?"

Annabelle squeals with excitement. "Then we can come here anytime we want."

"Anytime we want," I echo.

Chapter 15

SCARLETT

It's still not enough!

A groan slips from my lips, and I throw myself back into my chair as I stare at the spreadsheets before me. Even with three skate nights behind me, the skating lessons, and the uptick in skaters during the weeknights, I'm still short what I need if I want a chance at changing the bank's mind.

Maybe asking Kasper for help wouldn't be such a bad idea... now that we're dating.

Except how would that make me look?

Like I'm a gold-digger.

He offered. I'd just be accepting the offer he made before.

I shut my eyes and drag my hands down my face. My mind is at war with itself, and I don't know how to fix it. What I have with Kasper is too new. I can't ask him now. What would it do to our budding relationship? Especially since he plans to move here.

He's planning to move here.

The moan that escapes me makes my throat sore.

A prince from some country I've never heard of wants to move to a tiny town in Idaho because of me. The thought both electrifies and terrifies me at once. It's all too much to handle.

I think back to when I turned Kasper down the first time. I'd been stubborn and maybe a little too cocky for my own good. If I had just accepted his offer, then I wouldn't be dealing with unbalanced spreadsheets.

I might also not be kinda dating the guy.

My office door bursts open, and Holly breezes into the room before placing a to-go coffee cup on my paperwork. She unceremoniously settles into the chair across from me, her eyes sparkling with joy.

"I heard Prince Charming might be moving to Breckenridge."

My eyes widen, and I sit upright. I haven't told a soul about his plans to avoid jinxing the whole thing. "He told you?"

She shakes her head with a laugh. "But it's true? I thought it was a rumor. Meredith said her realtor friend was talking to a handsome man with brown hair and the most gorgeous brown eyes she's ever seen. He dresses like he's got money, and he's got a budget to back it up." Holly tilts her head and laughs as I continue to gape at her. "Does his decision to stay have something to do with that little skating lesson you gave him at the beginning of the week?"

I blink a few times, hating how my flushed cheeks give me away once again. "I don't know that's the reason per se."

Holly laughs. "You need to get a better poker face, you know that?" She leans forward. "So dish. If he's looking at property, what does that mean? He's getting a vacation home? He's settling down here for good?"

Shaking my head, I laugh with her. "You're a terrible gossip."

"I'm not a gossip. I've said nothing to anyone. It's Meredith you can blame this time. Just be grateful Eve hasn't heard."

"Why should I worry if our local baker has heard the latest on Kasper Montgomery?"

Holly shoots me a sly smile.

"Holly!" I laugh with exasperation. "What does Eve have to do with any of this?"

She shrugs her shoulders and brings her own cup to her lips to take a sip of her coffee. "Maybe because she's convinced she's the one playing matchmaker."

My eyes narrow, and my brows furrow. "Eve didn't introduce us."

Holly shakes her head. "Nope."

"That doesn't make her a matchmaker, then."

I watch as my friend snickers and rolls her eyes when I still don't catch on. "You remember the story about Breckenridge, right? About the magic well?"

It's my turn to roll my eyes as I lean back in my seat and wrap my cold hands around the warm cup. "You can't seriously believe in that stuff. We don't even have a well anymore. It was destroyed by some natural disaster."

"And Eve believes that her bakery was built over the top of it. How much do you want to bet that if we pulled up the blueprints for that place, it'd be drawing water from an ancient well?"

I grow still. It's a silly story, and anyone who believes it is asinine. But something about Holly's words tug at my heart. "And you think that Eve is using her baked goods to match people up?"

Holly lifts a shoulder. "What do you think?"

"I think you're nuts."

"Nope. But there are plenty of goodies in Stella's bakery that might contribute to such a disposition."

Our laughter fills my office, momentarily chasing away the cold disappointment of the state of my life. It's not all bad, I remind myself. Right now, my love life has much improved.

We're quiet for a moment, lost in thought. Holly tilts her head, her eyes getting a far-off look to them. "Come to think of it..." She shakes her head, her voice trailing off.

"What?" I ask.

She snickers. "You really will think I'm crazy."

"Go for it. Can't be any worse than I think of you now."

Her disgruntled look stirs another smile. Holly leans forward and places her cup on my desk. "Remember how I met Lucian?"

I nod. "You were staying at his bed and breakfast."

"Yep. And you want to know where my favorite thing to snack on while I was here came from?"

I roll my eyes. "Don't say Stella's."

"Stella's," she murmurs at the same time I do.

"Holly! You can't seriously be thinking that because you ate sweets from Stella's that you were destined to fall in love with Lucian. It's not realistic."

"Maybe not. But it's a cute idea. I'd like to think everything happens for a reason. Fate. Serendipity. Whatever you want to call it, I think it exists, and if we're listening, I believe it finds us."

I gesture to my paperwork. "And *this*? Discovering I've been hurt by someone I trusted? Was *that* fate?"

My friend frowns. "Of course not."

"Well, you can't have one without the other. I don't believe in fate. I believe that if you work hard at something and fight for your dreams, you get what you deserve. I wasn't on the ball with my manager, so I lost out. Plain and simple."

"Scarlett—"

"Don't." I place my cup on the table and rest my hands in front of me. "I'm not trying to be a Debbie Downer. I'm just stating facts. If I get out of this, it won't be because I was lucky. It's because I worked my butt off and found a way through it."

Holly leans forward and places a hand over mine. She squeezes my fingers, offering me as much comfort as she can give me. "And if I know you, it's going to happen."

I LET HOLLY GET IN MY HEAD.

That's the only explanation for why I'm even allowing myself to consider asking Kasper for help after I turned him down time and again. The only thing holding me back now is the fact that he hasn't offered again.

He hasn't pressed the issue, and at this point, I don't feel like I can bring it up.

Kasper is trying to buy property here. He may be royalty, but even royal money can only go so far.

What we have—it's different somehow. I don't want to risk any of it.

He smiles at me from where he's chatting with the mayor a little way down the street. Annabelle is distracted with the sweets in Stella's window. And all I can think about is regret for not letting Kasper help in the first place.

I force a smile, watching him return his focus to the mayor. It'd be hypocritical if I ask him for help after our relationship status has changed. That's what I keep telling myself. If I can't accept help from a stranger, I definitely can't accept it from someone I'm dating.

Dating.

The word is foreign in my own head.

Is that what's happening right now? I've spent time with Kasper and his daughter every single day for nearly a week. And we have plans to see each other right up until he leaves.

He's literally trying to move here.

Warmth starts in my chest and creeps across my skin. I look down at the adorable girl staring at candied fruits. The blueberries, strawberries, and raspberries literally look like they've been frozen into a ball of glass, but I know better. They're coated with a hard sugar shell. I don't blame the girl for her fascination with them. They are some of the prettiest things in the window display.

When I glance over at Kasper again, the mayor is gone, but the man I'm falling for is on the phone instead. His brows are creased, and he actually looks upset. Even when we butted heads upon meeting one another, he never looked so put out.

Kasper paces, then rakes a hand through his hair. I can hear his voice, but I can't make out the words he's saying. What can possibly be bad enough for him to get riled up about?

Moving.

My heart plummets. It's the only thing that makes sense. Either he's not finding the place he wants to purchase, or his family is pushing back against his request to move out here. If I were a betting woman, I'd assume the latter.

I swallow hard and force my gaze to Annabelle when she straightens. "I think I want some of those."

I don't have to look to know what she's pointing at.

"I'm sure your father will be happy to get them when he's done with his phone call."

Annabelle glances in her father's direction and frowns. "Why does he look upset?"

"I don't know sweetie. Probably grown-up stuff."

She stares for a moment longer, then nods. "Yeah. He has a lot of grown-up stuff he worries about."

"He does?"

Her innocent, angelic face peers up at me, and she nods again. "When we're at home, he gets frustrated a lot with work. I don't think he likes it."

I gnaw on the inside of my cheek. From what Kasper had said about his responsibilities, he isn't busy. So why did his daughter make it sound as though he's got more on his plate than he wants?

All at once, my sinking heart crumbles. I should have known better than to believe everything would work out. It isn't working out with my rink. And whatever this is that we have—it won't work out either. I feel utterly stuck. The sensation is suffocating. The way he looks right now is more than a good reason not to broach the subject regarding my business. If he's got a lot on his plate, the last thing he needs is to hear my concerns about the rink.

The weight of everything going on right now presses on me to the point that I don't hear him approaching. A gentle hand on the small of my back has me nearly jumping out of my skin. "Sorry I took so long. I got caught up with a call." His warm breath skitters across the back of my neck, and I shiver. These next few days may be the last few where I still have everything I never knew I want.

When Kasper leaves, it may be for good.

I smile, turning to him and placing a gloved hand to his cheek. "Your daughter has a bigger sweet tooth than I do. She's eyeing those sugared fruits."

He tears his focus from me to look at what I'm pointing to. "Well, at least it's somewhat healthy. Come on bug, let's get you a treat."

They enter the shop, and I linger outside, steeling myself for the inevitable. I can do this. I'm strong. Even if I end up losing everything, I will appreciate what I have.

Chapter 16

KASPER

My brother must be a bigger coward than I give him credit for. More calls. More requests to come home. He's even taken to arguing with me about staying longer—something I'm seriously considering.

But still, he won't give me a good reason to return besides the same old thing. My responsibilities. I can't help but roll my eyes every time I see a new message on my phone. I never knew my baby brother could be so relentless.

Today I fully intend on shutting my phone off and ignoring everything except Scarlett.

I flash her a smile as she exits the rink, Annabelle in tow. "You two ready to go?"

Scarlett's face scrunches up, and she releases a laugh. "Go? Where?"

"It's a surprise."

She gestures around the rink. "I've got things to do here. I have one more skate night to prepare for."

"It's not going to be all day." I have to get her out to the property. All I need is a little input from Ash Mathews before I make an offer. And there's nothing I want more than to have Scarlett by my side through it all. I wasn't lying when I told her I plan on moving out here. Nothing is going to stop me from making that dream come true.

Annabelle turns to Scarlett, her face bright with excitement. "Will you come? Daddy has the best surprises."

Before Scarlett can ask, I shake my head. "No, I haven't told her about the surprise either."

Her eyes swim with a palpable anticipation. Under normal circumstances, the way we're moving would be too fast. I know I'd be scaring her off. But something's different. I'm different when I'm with her. And somehow, I think she feels the same way.

Annabelle hobbles on her skates to the bench. She begins to unlace her skates while Scarlett waits on the edge of the ice. Her arm is draped over the wall's edge, and she tilts her head as I drift closer to her. "A surprise, huh? Does this have anything to do with you leaving in the next week?"

I reach for her face, grasping it in my hand as I trace my thumb across her cheek. Her skin is smooth and cool to the touch. If we didn't have an audience only a few feet away, I wouldn't hesitate to tilt her face so her lips could meet mine. Annabelle has taken to noticing the way I touch Scarlett, and I'm not ready for her to see us become that intimate so soon.

Scarlett leans into my touch, and I grin at her, allowing my frustration with James to flit away. "Yes, a surprise. And no, it has nothing to do with my scheduled flight back home."

She closes her eyes, and I can almost see the lines of worry form. It's not so much visible as it's something I can feel. She's on edge. Something's bothering her. I open my mouth to ask, but Annabelle speaks first.

"All done! Miss Scarlett, you need to get your shoes on. Hurry."

Scarlett's eyes open, and she laughs. "Okay, okay. I'm coming."

I stand back and let her pass, reveling in the way her presence can ease all the tension I carry.

"THE FROSTED WONDERLAND!" ANNABELLE practically shouts from her seat in the cab. If she wasn't buckled, I bet she'd be on her feet. "I love this place." She's sitting between Scarlett and me, her excited eyes drinking everything in. It's not dark yet. No lights are shining, but the venue itself is still impressive.

"Stay here, this is only a stop." I push the door open as Ash exits from a modest house off to the side of the property. He's dressed in boots and a heavy coat, and he's pulling on his gloves as he strides toward us. "Thanks for coming." I hold out a hand, and he takes it in a firm grasp. I don't have to look behind me to know that the occupants of the cab are watching us intently.

Ash glances over to the vehicle and smirks. "Have you told them?"

I shake my head. "I thought it best if it was a surprise. And only you can bring the vision to life."

"I don't know about that."

I clap him on the back and chuckle. "You say that now, but look at what you built, and with ice no less. I'm sure you are more than capable at helping me see this project through."

"Well, let's get to it then. I've got to get back here before dusk so I can have it open on time." Ash moves past me toward the waiting cab. He settles into the passenger seat, and I return to my spot beside my daughter.

Scarlett shoots me a curious glance, and I wink at her. There aren't many times in my life when I've felt completely at peace with a decision I've made. There are always so many variables to consider when planning for my future—for Annabelle's future. But this one? I know I'm on the right track. Nothing will stop me from giving Annabelle the life I know she deserves—the life we both do.

Annabelle continues to sit tall in her seat as if she expects to recognize where we're going, but I haven't breathed a word to her about the property I found. The small cottage will be a perfect place to stay while I build a house of our dreams.

I flex my hands. I can't remember a time I've been this nervous. What if Scarlett doesn't like my idea? Would it matter? I knew this place was special from the moment we arrived. Would I still want to stay if Scarlett wasn't part of my plans?

Deep down I know my nerves come from wanting to share that special feeling with *her*.

I can feel her eyes on me, and it takes all my self-control not to look in her direction.

I need to calm my nerves.

"Here we are."

I lean forward and hand the cab driver my card. "Keep it running. We shouldn't be more than twenty minutes."

The man nods, and I steal a glance at Scarlett.

She's staring at the quaint little cottage in front of us. So is Annabelle. Ash has already exited the vehicle, and he's moving toward the entrance.

"There's a for sale sign out front," Scarlett whispers. "I didn't think you were serious."

I nod, watching her closely as she slowly swivels her head to face me.

"Are you buying this place?"

Annabelle gasps. "Are we?"

I chuckle, the sound strained and cracking. "How about we go out there and talk to Ash for a minute?" I can feel my palms growing clammier by the second. Suddenly, this decision sounds really dumb. I can hear James's criticism on this matter, running the rounds in my head. If he was here, seeing what I'm about to do, he'd do his best to get the crown to cut me off.

Shaking off that thought, I walk around the cab to take Scarlett's hand in mine. She's still staring at the house with wonder. At least she doesn't seem to be upset with my impulsive decision.

Ash turns to face us, his eyes lingering on Scarlett for a moment. There's a curiosity in his gaze more than anything else. But he doesn't say what's on his mind. He runs a hand back and forth over his hair, then points to the house. "Whether you decide to keep the house or not won't really matter in the long run."

"Whether you decide to keep it?" Scarlett echoes. "Are you going to demolish it?"

I lift a shoulder. "Ash is here to give me an idea of what we can do with this property. Ideally, I'd like something big enough to start a family... eventually." I watch her closely, but I can't read any reaction. "He's got experience with building cabins. His father was a logger, and he's gone to college for architecture."

She turns her wide eyes to me. "You're serious." Her breath comes out in a soft puff, and I can't hide the smile that touches my lips.

"Deadly." I squeeze her hand, thrilled that she's not pulling away. "Now, I know that we've only just started dating. And I'm not asking you for a commitment by any means." My words stick in my throat as I try to come up with the explanation I had in my head. "I brought you here so you could see that I'm serious. I want to see where things might go between us. There's potential here, and I'm not willing to risk losing it by trying to maintain it long distance. I hope... that's okay?"

Scarlett doesn't move, and I can feel Ash's curious stare. I haven't told him anything about myself beyond being a foreigner. Knowing too much could prove problematic in so many ways.

I squeeze her hand again, and she finally glances toward me. "Please tell me you don't think I'm crazy."

She releases a little laugh and shakes her head. "Oh, you're definitely a little crazy. But if you are, so am I." Leaning closer to me, her smile widens. "You're going to build yourself a castle, aren't you?"

I chuckle. "I wouldn't go that far."

Ash jerks his chin toward the house. "Let's see what we've got behind here, and I can give you a better idea of what we will need to do to prepare for a build."

I wag my brows at Scarlett. "You interested?"

"I don't think I've been more interested in my entire life."

***

My laughter bubbles out of my throat as I walk around the cab to open the door for Scarlett on the other side. On the ride back, Annabelle can't stop asking about what her room will look like and whether I'll give her a playset or a pool.

There are even a few moments when my eyes meet Scarlett's and it actually feels like we're planning a future together—past the end of this month.

"Kasper? Where on earth have you been?"

I stiffen. That voice. I don't have to turn toward the bed and breakfast to know who is standing on its premises. Slowly, I turn, and James's angry face comes into view.

He looks utterly exhausted. His brown hair is mussed, and his suit is disheveled. If I didn't know any better, I would assume that he took a commercial flight to get here.

James strides down the steps toward me, and Annabelle squeals with excitement. "Uncle James!" She throws her arms around his waist, causing him to stumble and slow, but his fiery gaze is still locked and loaded on me.

"Hey, bug?"

Annabelle turns toward me.

"Will you take Scarlett inside with you? I'm sure Meredith can fix you up some lunch before we have to take Scarlett back to the rink."

As expected, Annabelle's excitement only grows. She scurries back to Scarlett's side and tugs on her hand to take her toward the entrance. As soon as the cab pulls away and there are no burning ears to hear our conversation, I set a dark look on my brother.

"Well, it's got to be really bad if you braved the flight to come all the way here. So, are you finally going to tell me what's going on?"

James's face is red, almost comically so. I'd laugh if I wasn't so upset about him showing up unannounced. No one knows I'm a prince—except Scarlett. Well, and I'm assuming Holly and her husband. I don't even think Meredith knows entirely.

I cross my arms, waiting for James to confess. It's got to come out at some point.

James runs a hand through his hair and glances back at the building. "I shouldn't have had to come to get you."

"You wouldn't have had to if you'd told me what's going on."

Still, I see his hesitation plain as day. I'm beginning to think he won't say a word when he heaves a sigh and shakes his head.

"Alex is sick."

Chapter 17

SCARLETT

"Sweetie, how about you go tell Meredith we're going to need a really yummy lunch, okay?" I give Annabelle a little push into the bed and breakfast. My heart is thundering for reasons I'm not making sense of. Uncle James. The man outside is Kasper's brother. Is he the older one? Or the younger one?

It really shouldn't matter. He's here to speak to Kasper, which means something is wrong.

I spin around and hurry to the window that faces the front of the property. I can't see James's face, but based on how stiff he looks, I know in my gut he's not visiting for pleasure. Dark, accusatory eyes fill my mind from when I first caught sight of him. He hadn't been looking at me, but the memory burns in my mind.

Kasper is scowling right back at his brother, an air of defiance in his stance. His chin is cocked, his arms folded. I can already imagine him telling his brother where to shove it before he pushes past him to return to my side.

But he doesn't.

Slowly, his features change.

The hard planes in his face shift, and an excruciating pain fills his eyes. His jaw slackens, and he takes a step toward his brother, shaking his head. I can hear him yelling, but I can't make out the words he's saying. He flings his arms in the air and paces, shaking his head.

James is yelling too.

The knots in my stomach coil and tighten, weakening me from the inside out. My hands grip the windowsill as I lean forward. This isn't good. I can already tell something bad is going to happen. It is happening, and there's nothing I can do to change course.

I turn, leaning my back against the wall that frames the window. Clutching my neck with trembling fingers, I close my eyes and focus on taking a deep breath. I know what's happening. As much as I want to try to convince myself otherwise, I know.

Kasper won't be coming back.

I shouldn't be surprised.

Heck, I shouldn't even be hurting.

It's not logical to fall in love with a man after knowing him for three weeks. I'm the insane one. And yet a tear slips from the corner of my eye. I feel like my world is crumbling. He's not my soul mate. There's no such thing as magic or a magic well. And yet I find myself wanting to blame my attachment to this prince on those very notions. What am I thinking?

"Miss Scarlett? Are you okay?"

My eyes fly open, and I find Annabelle frowning up at me. She won't know that she's not coming back for a while. I can already see the way Kasper may try to put off telling her, and I can't be the one to make her dreams come crashing down.

Forcing a smile, I crouch in front of her and help her remove her coat. "I'm fine. Just a little dizzy is all."

Her adorable little brow creases as she never breaks eye contact with me. One arm out, then the other. I hold her black peacoat out to her. "Where does Meredith like you to put this?"

Annabelle doesn't take it right away. Her eyes shift to the window where I was standing, and her frown deepens. "Is Uncle James mad?"

Silence surrounds us except for the pulse roaring in my ears. What am I supposed to say to that? I can tell James is mad. It isn't hard to see. But I can't tell her. She's not my daughter.

And she never will be.

That voice strikes me hard, and I suck in a breath. When did I become so blinded to these feelings I have for this little family? One moment it was nothing, and the next I'm faltering in everything I know.

"I think your uncle has been trying to get ahold of your father, and he's been ignoring him."

"Why?"

I shake my head. "I don't know, sweetie. But sometimes grownups make choices they think are best. You'll have to ask your daddy when he comes inside."

As if in response to my statement, the door swings open. I half expect to see the men coming inside together, but the only one who enters is Kasper. He looks whiter than he did outside. Slowly, I rise to my feet and face him. "Is your brother… okay?"

Kasper's eyes dart to me, then Annabelle, then me again. "Annabelle, sweetheart, I need to talk to Miss Scarlett for a moment. Go see if Meredith can use your help."

Annabelle frowns. I can see the hesitation and worry in her eyes. The child is usually so accommodating without any second thoughts. But this time, she doesn't move. "Is Uncle James mad at you?"

Cold seeps into the room, permeating my bones. Kasper lets out a burst of breath through pursed lips. He glances at me again and rubs his neck. This is more than an angry brother—just like I had predicted.

They won't be staying long, and I hate how that makes my heart break a little bit more.

I expect him to say that, to tell Annabelle they're going to leave earlier than planned. Instead, he forces out a chuckle and a smile to go with it. "It's nothing serious, kiddo. I just want to talk to Scarlett for a minute."

No one in the room can possibly believe the man. The worry in his face is etched deep. But Annabelle nods and wanders toward the kitchen, tossing her father one more fleeting glance over her shoulder.

"What's happened?" I demand the second he looks at me.

He chuckles again. The sound grates against my frayed nerves. "Just James overreacting to something back home. I'll handle it when I head back. Nothing has changed."

"That conversation certainly didn't look like nothing," I mutter against my own best judgement. I didn't want him to realize I was watching them. He asked for privacy, and I didn't exactly give it.

Betrayal and surprise flicker across his countenance as his eyes cut to me. He wants to ask me if I heard anything. Or he may want to reprimand me for putting my nose where it doesn't belong. What right do I have to insert myself into his family affairs?

None.

None whatsoever.

I steel myself for that very argument between us, but all he does is move toward me and pull me closer to him. My chest crushes against his as he holds me in a tight hug. My muscles are stiff, not from the cold but from the sense I get that he's holding so much back from me.

What secrets were discussed between him and his brother? He's not being honest with me. He's not telling me the important parts.

Once again, I remind myself that I can't do anything about it. We've only just started our relationship. And I hate that I'm not confident enough to push him to open up more.

Loneliness.

It's ironic, because in this very moment, Kasper is holding me close. He's brushing his lips to the top of my head and rubbing his hands along my back.

But right now, all I feel is this desperate loneliness. I can't shake it.

Kasper knows everything about me. He's heard the worst of my fears, and he's there for me. Why won't he allow me to be the same thing for him?

My high from earlier today is officially smothered. When Meredith arrives in the foyer with Annabelle on her heels announcing grilled cheese and tomato soup, I can't force my appetite to return.

Soon, we're all seated around a table, steaming bowls of soup accompanying the most delicious grilled cheese I've ever looked at. Three different kinds of cheese melt between two slices of fresh sourdough bread.

And yet?

I don't think I can keep it down if I try.

Tension continues to mount, though thankfully, Annabelle doesn't seem to notice. She's happily munching on her sandwich as she chatters about what Santa may bring her all the way in Idaho.

I can feel Kasper's concerned stare on me as I take small nibbles of my own sandwich. Pinching off the crust between my finger and thumb, I study it for a moment before pushing it between my lips.

James's arrival means something. I know it. There's only one reason why he'd make the trip. Something is up, and Kasper is in denial.

"Is the sandwich okay?" Meredith's voice shatters my musings, and I glance up at her.

I force a smile. "It's delicious."

Great. Now all eyes are on me. Kasper slows his eating. Annabelle completely stops. And poor Meredith clasps her hands tightly in front of her while she watches me from behind the reservation desk. Her eyes are creased with worry, mirroring Kasper's. If I don't put on a happy face, I'm sure I'll be dragged out of this room and forced to share exactly what's bothering me.

The smile I paste on doesn't feel right, even to me. It's foreign and almost hurts. But I power through it. "I'm so sorry. I wasn't very hungry. I should have told you before you made it."

Meredith's expression relaxes, but only slightly. "Well, dear. Obviously, you don't have to finish it. I can box it up for you, and you can reheat it for supper." She moves across the room and holds out her hand.

The temptation to bring the plate to my chest and prevent her from doing that tears at me. As if my fingers don't get the memo of my thoughts, they tighten on the plate right before Meredith takes it from my hands.

Heat crawls along my skin, evidence that I know I failed miserably in showing my manners to the kind woman who fixed me some lunch.

I don't bring my eyes around to look at Kasper. I know I'll see that same concern in his eyes. I know he won't be able to let it go. He's going to want to ask me what's wrong. In the end, I'll say something dumb like I know he's lying about his brother.

Darting to my feet, I turn in the direction Meredith has taken and wait. The second she returns, I accept the bag of food she presents. "Thank you," I whisper.

Meredith's smile is genuine, but it still doesn't give me the peace my heart seeks.

That's when I hear scuffling, and I turn to find Kasper standing. He's got a napkin in his fingertips at his side. His food is half-eaten. His jaw is set in a hard line, but his eyes beseech me to talk to him. Annabelle simply looks curious.

One side of my mouth lifts upward, and tears spring behind my eyes.

I will not cry.

Crying over a relationship this new is silly.

And as far as Kasper is concerned, nothing is wrong.

Bitterness pools within me.

Nothing is wrong.

"I'll see you later?" I can't help the question that lifts the final word.

Kasper steps toward me. I shake my head slightly, not wanting to draw more attention to the fact that I'm dealing with something I can't find the words for. He stops.

Sweet, sweet Annabelle nods. "Can we do some more ice-skating just for fun?"

My eyes dart to hers, and my smile widens. "Of course, sweetheart."

Then I leave, feeling empty and more alone than I did at the beginning of the month.

Chapter 18

KASPER

I don't know how Scarlett knows, but she does. Has she been eavesdropping?

No.

I don't believe she'd violate my privacy like that.

Scarlett may not know exactly what's going on, but she's smart enough to know I'm blatantly lying to her when I say nothing will change.

Honestly, I don't know if anything will change or if everything will.

I lace my fingers behind my head and charge back and forth in the bedroom I share with Annabelle.

She's coloring now, completely oblivious to what's going on.

Alexander is terminally ill.

Stage four of something I wouldn't be able to pronounce right if I wanted to. James shattered my world with that announcement. For the last couple of weeks, he'd simply made excuse after excuse about why I needed to come home. He'd avoided the topic so many times, I'd grown tired of it. And he'd merely insisted it was something I had to be told in person.

I could hate him for that. But I hated myself more. I knew something was wrong and I didn't heed my brother's request.

I shut my eyes, trying to imagine the pain and fear my oldest brother is dealing with at home.

My parents! What they must be going through!

I want to cry. No, I want to throw things, be destructive, get out all this pent-up energy that has suddenly seeped into my bones and currently flows through every vein in my body.

But I can't.

Annabelle won't understand. Heck, I'm not sure if she truly understands the concept of death, even after she lost her mother. Part of me wonders if she doesn't believe she'll see her mother again one day. Can a child that young understand heaven in the traditional sense?

I blow out a breath, pausing to watch her. She loves her uncles. And she's already lost so much. More death. More loss. I can't bring myself to tell her. Not yet. I need her innocence to last a little longer.

"Alex is sick."

I snort. "What do you mean? Does he have the flu? I hardly think that's any reason for me to come home early. He'll be fine."

"Cancer. Glioblastoma multiforme. Stage four. It spread quickly, and it's lethal. The doctors say he doesn't have long."

It's cold outside, but my insides are colder. I can't move. My lungs have seized up and refuse to operate.

No. It's not true. I refuse to believe it.

Alex was fine when I left. He was planning and preparing for the holidays and every ridiculous event he was required to attend. He had a fiancée but no kids. What would happen to the line of succession?

Then it hits me.

The air seeps back into my lungs with a sharpness that I can't be entirely certain doesn't involve prickly ice crystals.

"No."

James lifts his brows. "No?"

"I won't do it."

My brother snorts derisively. "You don't have a choice. You know what happens in royal families. You're the next in line."

"I will abdicate, then."

"What?" he snaps.

"I mean it. I don't want the throne. I never have. I'd rather walk out of our country with only the clothes on my back than be forced to lead."

"Don't be so dramatic," he mutters. "It's not as bad as all that."

"Then you do it."

This time James laughs. "It's not that easy, and you know it."

"Do I? Think about it, James. You're better suited for that lifestyle anyway. I have zero interest and I would be... terrible."

He huffs, an agreement to my statement, but all the while he shakes his head. "Mother and father won't accept that."

"They won't have a choice. If I have to stay here for the rest of my life, I will."

He glances toward the bed and breakfast where Scarlett disappeared with Annabelle. "She's beautiful, I give you that."

"She's not the reason."

"Isn't she? I could have sworn you were planning on moving here the first chance you got."

I scowl at him. While I had alluded to the fact that I wanted to get some property out here, I hadn't confessed to moving out here permanently. I'm not sure how he managed to figure it out, but he has. There's no use denying it. At this point, my whole family already knows.

James heaves a sigh. "Look, I know you haven't canceled your flight yet. Come home. Say goodbye to Alex. Hear him out. Listen to your parents. Then make a decision."

"So now I get a decision?"

My baby brother actually rolls his eyes. No, he doesn't believe I have a choice. But he'll see. I refuse to allow people to dictate my life for me. I've been overlooked for far too long. Now, I'm going to take full advantage of it and take what I want out of life.

The conversation runs on repeat in my head. Even as my final thoughts while in my brother's company flood my mind, I know I'm wrong to believe everything will work out the way I want it to.

I wish I'd told Scarlett.

That look on her face ripped through me like the frigid winter wind outside. It left me breathless and praying she doesn't shut me out until I can explain better.

I stop my pacing.

It was a mistake to let her go without telling her what's going on. She deserves to know—mostly because James is closer to being right than I am.

There's a lot that would need to go into shifting the responsibilities to James. The fact that he is the youngest of the three of us would make things very messy.

And bringing Scarlett into this?

I already know my parents would far prefer for me to court Scarlett long distance and bring her into the fold. That's just how they are.

How can I ask her to do such a thing? Nothing would make me happier than to see her be part of my family in the country I love. But doing so is akin to taking a lion from the Sahara and putting it behind glass in a zoo.

Scarlett would never be happy living a life like that one, and I care far too much about her to even ask.

Still, she needs to know what's really happening—and from me, rather than someone else.

MY HAND TIGHTENS AROUND SCARLETT'S. I COULD TELL she wasn't thrilled to see me when I showed up at the end of the evening as she started locking up. It took about five minutes of convincing her to go for a quiet, moonlit walk with me.

Her wary gaze says it all.

Just like when she left the bed and breakfast, her body language gives her away. She's already retreated from me—walls are erected.

I clear my throat. "I wasn't completely honest with you," I murmur.

"Really?" Sarcasm laces her words, and I flinch.

"I could make excuse after excuse, but I won't. It doesn't

matter my reasons. I should have told you what James came by to say."

"Is he gone?"

I sigh. "Yes. He left the country shortly after our conversation."

She lifts her brows, and the animosity that lingers in her eyes slips away slowly. "Oh. I'm sorry."

I release a bitter laugh. "You don't have anything to be sorry about."

The air grows still between us. Unspoken words. Soon to be broken promises. As much as I wish to read the future, I can't, and I have to be okay with that.

"My brother is sick."

"James?"

I shake my head. "Alex. My older brother."

"Is he going to be okay?" Her genuine concern warms my bitter soul.

"No." That one word weighs on us—heavy, unyielding, and painful. Tears threaten me once again.

I'm losing so much. My family. My freedom. The girl of my dreams.

At least that's how it feels.

"What does that mean... for you?"

I shut my eyes, blocking out the beautiful evening. I can't bring myself to look at the stars or the glowing streetlamps that illuminate the freshly fallen snow from the afternoon. I can't bear to listen to the quiet music floating through the small town. Christmas melodies that I may not hear from these sidewalks ever again. "I don't know."

"You don't know?" she asks far too quickly.

Stopping, I face her and frame her face with my gloved hands. "I'm scheduled to go home at the end of the week. The day after Christmas. If I go home, there's a strong possibility that I won't be permitted to return here."

She does an excellent job at keeping her expression cool. No shock. No pain. No longing.

What is she thinking?

I bite back the desire to demand her to speak.

Scarlett merely blinks, and I blink back.

"If I go home, our relationship—I know it will suffer. I don't want that to happen." It's a leading statement. A cowardly way for me to nudge her in the direction I want.

Tell me you love me.

Tell me you want to come with me.

Tell me you'll walk away from everything you've ever known so you can be my future queen.

The words sound so romantic in my head, and at the same time, so utterly confining.

Freedom. That's what I want for her. That's what she deserves.

"And if you don't go?"

"If I don't go," I hedge, then release a strained chuckle. "I might be dragged back anyway. I might be left alone and disowned by my family. Who's to say?"

She seems to consider my words. The amount of time she takes to mull them over is excruciating. Finally, she lifts her chin slightly. "I know you'll make the right decision." Scarlett's words are a shock to my system. So many other responses would have been easier to swallow. If she broke up with me, for instance, I'd be able to accept it. If she insisted we'd be okay, I'd let out a holler of joy. But to tell me to make the life-defining decision? What did she expect me to say to that?

"What does that even mean?" I hear myself whispering.

Scarlett lifts her shoulders and drops them, her hands coming up to grasp my wrists as she pulls them from her face. "I can't make the decision for you. This is your life."

"It's *our* life," I snap, my voice sharper than intended.

But she doesn't flinch. She doesn't react.

And I'm beginning to wonder if she feels remotely the same for me as I do for her. Maybe I had this all wrong from the start. It would make sense that I interpreted her affection as something bigger. It's been so long since I had someone to call my own. Did I see more when there is none?

My stomach tilts on its side. I have to close my eyes briefly to avoid the dizziness I'm feeling. For the first time in a long time, I feel truly and utterly alone.

Ridiculous as that may seem.

When I lost Rose, I didn't feel this alone. I had my family to hold me up. But right here, right now, when I want nothing more than to have Scarlett help me through this, she refuses me.

I swallow hard, nodding.

She's right, of course. As painful as it is, I need to decide for myself what I want.

I'm just not sure where she'll stand after I make my choice, and that terrifies me.

I open my mouth to say as much, but she stops me with a finger to my lips.

"Thank you for telling me."

It's a strange thing for her to say. I want more. I need her to tell me that she cares about me like I do for her.

"I should get going."

Once again, she leaves me speechless. Scarlett's eyes study mine, bouncing back and forth. It's dark enough I can't tell if she's about to cry. She certainly appears to need the release. If I pull her into my arms and promise that I love her, will she stay with me?

Before I can get the words to spill from my lips, she pecks me on the cheek and hurries away.

Chapter 19

SCARLETT

I can only remember feeling this hollow one other time in my life, and it happened a few weeks ago. Each step I take toward the rink feels like I'm going to collapse.

This isn't normal.

It can't be.

Just because Kasper is charming—and a prince, no less—doesn't mean that I'm forever changed by the man.

Besides, nothing is over yet.

He's been presented with a choice. And he can choose me.

Will he choose me?

My world is officially crumbling. At the edges of my mind, I can see bits and pieces of what I thought was reality shifting until it no longer looks the same.

The rink is slipping through my fingers. I definitely can't ask Kasper for help now. He may very well be leaving for good.

He may be king one day.

Bitterness churns in my stomach, reminding me that I avoided eating lunch and skipped dinner all together. I'm going to be sick.

Why do I feel like I was pushing him away in our last conversation? I didn't tell him to leave. Heck, it took every ounce of determination and stubbornness to clamp my mouth shut when what I really wanted to do was beg him to take me with him.

I make it home in a daze, but sleep eludes me while I go over every single painstaking detail of that conversation. He didn't ask me to come with him. Why?

You didn't ask him to stay. Why didn't you do that?

Because he wouldn't have done it.

You don't know that.

I huff to myself, the argument in my mind taking front and center stage.

Why on earth would a family man like Kasper disown said family, all so he could stay here in this small town with a failing, retired ice-skater?

What do I have to offer him?

Truth be told, he deserves a queen—a regal woman who can stand beside him with her head held high—a woman who knows how to smile and wave and not embarrass him in public.

As much as I yearn to maintain this fairytale romance with Kasper, the thought of being in a royal family fills me with a new kind of bitterness. I don't want that responsibility—no matter how much I want to belong to Kasper and care for Annabelle.

What if that's the price you have to pay to keep them?

I hate that question. It's one I refuse to answer even in my head.

My life is already upended. The small apartment above the

rink will soon have to be cleared out. I'll be in search of another job.

Dreams shattered.

There's still a chance Kasper will choose you.

I close my eyes and let the darkness sweep me into a dreamless sleep. I'm not going to hold my breath for that possibility. While Kasper gave no indication that he had decided one route or the other, deep down I can feel it in my bones.

Nothing works out for me the way I want it to.

Time to accept that now.

※ ❄ ※

THE WEEK OF CHRISTMAS IS USUALLY SLOWER THAN the rest of the month at the rink. People are more focused on family get-togethers or last-minute shopping. I offer to hold lessons for those who are currently enrolled, but I finally accept that the rink is going to be taken from me.

The money I've raised simply isn't enough.

My clients are admittedly surprised by my announcement—besides Kasper. His expression remains stoic, if not a little hard.

After our little walk, I anticipated that he'd avoid me.

Unfortunately for him, Annabelle refuses to let that happen.

She has three more lessons this week.

Three more excruciating hours where Kasper sulks on the bleachers.

No word from him on his decision—just quiet brooding.

That, if anything, should give me my answer.

While a twisted part of me finds a little bit of joy in knowing I meant enough to him that he's upset about leaving, it's overshadowed by the realization that he's all but chosen the course he's going to take.

"Are you okay, Miss Scarlett?"

I drag my eyes from Kasper and pin them on his daughter. Shoot. I'm staring again. I need to stop doing that. Surely, he's tallying up each and every instance. I'm making a fool of myself.

A lump lodges in my throat, limiting my ability to speak clearly. My voice comes out squeaky and overflowing with emotion despite my best efforts. "I'm fine, sweetie."

Annabelle tilts her head and really watches me.

Sheesh, how can a girl so young look like she knows more about the universe than me?

"Are you mad at Daddy?"

My eyes fly wide, and my head whips around to stare at him, only to find him missing from his usual bench. Momentarily, I'm dazed from the whiplash, but I bring my focus back to Annabelle and lower my voce. "No. I'm not mad."

"Are you sad?"

That's a loaded question. How do I answer that without telling a bold-faced lie?

"I can tell you're sad," she answers for me, her eyes dropping to the ice. "Dad's sad too."

"He is?" More evidence that he's picking something he claimed he doesn't want.

She nods. "My uncle is sick."

I want to shake him. I want to march right up to that man and tell him it's not fair for him to use that as an excuse.

The second that thought filters though my muddled brain, I'm immediately swarmed by prickles of guilt. His brother is terminally sick. He's going to lose another member of his family. As hard as I feel my life has become, Kasper's is being turned upside down and shaken viciously.

I can't in good conscience be angry with him. There is no universe where I can even be disappointed in him or hold any grudges. His hands are tied.

In a swift movement, I fall to my knees in front of the cherub of a little girl and hold her hands. "He told me your uncle is sick."

She lifts her wet eyes to meet mine, and my heart shatters further. "He's going to die."

It's as if my tongue swells, full of lead or some other heavy material. I can't speak. I can't swallow. I don't know what I'm going to do to help this child through these emotions. Rationally, I know it's not my job. I'm just her teacher.

Just her teacher.

And yet some part of me wishes I could be more.

Alas, that will never happen. Perhaps if Kasper and I had more time together, no one could label what we have as merely a fling.

I shake off that notion the moment it materializes in my mind. I'm not cut out for a lifestyle change such as that one. Kasper knows it. I know it. No sense in dwelling.

I lift my knit-covered fingers to her cheek and dash away a tear that's slipped free. "Yes, sweetheart. He will."

She nods and brushes at another tear. "It will be okay, though. He's going to be with my mom."

I didn't think my heart could break any more than it already has. She's experienced so much loss, and yet here she stands, as strong as ever. Annabelle has had more loss than anyone should at her age. And I'm sitting here, allowing myself to succumb to tears because of what?

Losing my rink?

I should be ashamed of myself.

Swallowing hard, I offer her a smile. "That's a wonderful thought, isn't it?"

She nods. Without warning, she throws her arms around my shoulders, clinging to me as soft sobs rack her body. I vaguely hear the sound of footsteps approaching. Before I lift my gaze, he speaks.

"Is everything okay? I was just gone for a moment."

I drag my eyes to the man I fell in love with the first moment I saw him. He'd been infuriating, pushy, charming, and mesmerizing all at once. Never would I have predicted to feel so much for someone in such a short amount of time.

His eyes drill into me. The worry for his daughter is there, surely. But there's something more hovering in the darkness of his penetrating gaze. It's like he wants to say something—ask something?—that he can't find the words for.

I know that feeling intimately.

The longer I look at him, the more I come to the realization that it doesn't matter what he picks. If he chooses to stay, I need to push him away. He's got a family to worry about—a daughter who will need the support of her grandparents and other relatives. It's selfish and foolish to expect him to pick me over them.

And if he chooses to leave?

One day, I will get through it. One day, I will find someone who might come close to giving me what I had during the last few weeks.

I nod, my grip on his daughter tightening. "Everything is fine," I whisper.

No, it's not. But it will be.

The last shreds of my heart crumble to ash as I realize what I've decided.

I'm letting him go. He's going to leave, and I'm going to make sure that happens without incidents. I'll take the money I made and try to start fresh. Maybe I can still keep my job and work for whoever buys the rink after it sells.

My stomach roils when I think about that. I've been my own boss for so long, I'm not sure I remember how to take orders from someone else.

Annabelle pulls away and wipes at her face again. We share one more meaningful look, and she skates off the ice toward her father.

Kasper's eyes never leave mine. I still get the sense that he wants to say something, but then his gaze shifts. I can't put my finger on it exactly, but I know he can see my resolve. It's as if his own hopes have officially been destroyed.

I did that.

It's my fault.

If he needs someone to blame for the path his life will now take, then fine. I'll be the bad guy. I'll be the person who reminds him that we were never something serious—as much as the words will poison me.

There will be time for healing after he's gone.

I get to my feet and skate to the edge of the ice. My focus drops to the floor. I can't bring myself to look him in the eye before he leaves. Two more lessons. I don't think I'll be able to spend time with him the way we did when we had our futures open to us. It will only hurt.

I'll have to find excuses and ways to avoid him for the remainder of his trip.

You should break up with him now.

I can't. Annabelle wants those last few lessons, and I'd be lying if I said I didn't crave them just as much. I won't ruin that for her. She needs to feel as much normalcy as she can—whatever that looks like.

Kasper reaches out, and his hand grazes my arm when I pass. I don't stop. I can't. If I do, I know I'll crumble. So I keep my eyes trained forward as I make my way back to the front desk.

Chapter 20

KASPER

"You've had your fun. It's time to come home." James growls, pacing the front porch of the Gingerbread Cottage.

I watch him from where I lean against the door, arms folded. "I thought you went home."

He snaps a dark look at me. "Clearly I didn't."

"Does this mean you're being a hypocrite?"

This time, he stops his pacing and whirls to face me, face redder than a ripe tomato. If I wasn't so upset about Scarlett dodging my calls, I might have laughed.

The fact that she's avoiding me only makes me angrier. The only time I can track her down is at Annabelle's skating lesson. And there's no way for me to speak to her afterward because she's moved another kid into that time slot.

She's doing everything she can to prevent me from starting

another conversation about my leaving. Up until today, I was still undecided in my plans.

James is still staring at me like I've attempted to knock him over the head with one of those plastic candy cane decorations that litters the lawn. He's huffing and puffing. I bet he hates being our parents' errand boy.

"I told you. I'm not changing my flight."

"I have a private jet here waiting at the hangar. We can go whenever. You know as well as I do that money isn't an issue. What's keeping you here? That woman? You barely know her."

My eyes narrow on my brother. "How would you know?"

He groans. Hands fly to the air, and he's pacing again. "I can't believe I'm actually arguing with you on this. Alex is dying. We don't know how long he has left. And you're dragging your feet here... in Idaho of all places."

That statement digs at me more than I want him to know. He's right about one thing. Alex is my brother, and Scarlett is someone who has only turned my life upside down in the last couple of weeks. What kind of man does that make me that I would prioritize my visit rather than go home to see my dying brother?

I'm a terrible person.

My jaw works, the muscles ticking back and forth as I let the guilt sink in. With Scarlett avoiding me, she's practically given me her standing on the matter. She doesn't want to fight for us. I can't blame her. Who wants to be trapped with a man who's an ocean away from her? I've seen better odds with two people who legitimately hate each other.

Dragging a hand down my face, I pull away from the door and

shove my hands into my pockets. I can tell James that I'm staying for Annabelle's benefit, but he'll see through that lie in a second.

"I know you said you don't think they'd go for making you the next in line—"

His head whips around, and he glares at me again. "They won't."

"But would you want it?"

"It doesn't matter what I want," he snaps.

I lift a brow. Clearly, he does, even though he hasn't outright told me he thinks I'm a bad choice. If we're honest with each other, we all know that none of us really *wants* to be next in line. This is more of a matter of who would be a better fit.

James fits the bill. There's no denying it.

His expression softens slightly, and he moves closer to me. "All I'm asking is that you come home so we can work this out. Mom and Dad haven't announced anything yet. They need the family whole before they make their first move. It's getting harder to hide Alex's condition. And each passing day, he's getting worse."

That sickness in my stomach increases. I want to hate how right he is. I'm being selfish. It's time to face facts and let go of the dreams I found for myself while I was here.

It's time to go home.

"Fine," I mutter tonelessly.

His brows lifted. I can practically see the words forming in his head. *Just like that? Why are you giving in? Is there something I don't know?*

Yes. There's a lot he doesn't know. There's so much he doesn't know, and I won't deign to tell him a single thing. He doesn't deserve to know what I'm going through, how I finally found love again.

He'll never understand—not until he falls in love.

Love.

The word mocks me.

I've been lucky enough to find it twice now.

And both times, it's been ripped from my grasp.

"*Fine?*" James says the word slowly as if testing it out—perhaps worried that uttering the word will make me take it back.

"Fine," I repeat. "But I have to do a couple things before I go."

He arches a brow at me, and I smirk. I won't be telling him anything. He doesn't deserve to know.

Flicking my fingers toward him, I wave him off the porch. "Give me two days."

"Two days!" he snaps with exasperation. "Your original flight leaves in four."

"Do you want me to leave early or not?" I cross my arms and give him a dark look. I'm more than happy to stretch this out just to spite the man. He's the one reason my vacation has been less than ideal. From all the messages to all those phone calls, I've barely been able to relax like I'd hoped.

James mutters something beneath his breath, and I bite back a smile. I'll probably be ready to go in twenty-four hours. I only need to make a couple phone calls and stop by Stella's. Annabelle is going to be upset when she finds out she'll be missing one of her lessons, but she'll survive. She's strong.

Stronger than me.

I watch James head down the steps toward a dark sedan that's been parked out on the street for the duration of this visit before I stride down a side of the wrap-around porch and pull out my phone. I don't know if Ash will be happy about what I've decided to do. The property is still mine, but the money I put down for Ash to start building hasn't been touched.

His number is one of the top results in my recent calls. I tap his name, then lift the phone to my ear. I'm going to miss this town. It's like a real Christmas village everywhere I look. From the quaint storefronts to the Christmas festival, it's everything I wanted to share with Annabelle when I decided to bring her here.

The disappointment I share with my daughter over not being able to stay is so heavy that I've half a mind to go back on my agreement with James and hide until everyone thinks I've died.

I can't do that to Alex.

Nor can I do that to my parents.

"This is Ash," he mutters into the phone.

"Ash, it's Kasper. I need to talk to you about something."

He grunts. It sounds like he's busy working on something, but he's not going to hang up on me.

"You haven't purchased anything for the property, have you?"

"No. I can't get started until the new year. Most of the companies that sell the stuff I want are closed for the holiday—at least when purchasing the amount of supplies we need."

"Good." Is my voice actually strangled? I can't believe I sound like I'm breaking.

"Everything okay?"

I nod, then clear my throat. "Yes. I'm fine. But something's come up. I don't want you starting on the project."

"No problem. When would you like me to start?"

I hesitate. "That's what I'm calling you about. The thing is—I don't know." He's not aware that I'm royalty. All he knows is that I come from money and I have plenty of it to spend. Rubbing the back of my neck, I charge up and down the porch much like my brother did only moments before. "I'm not sure you will be."

More silence. I can practically hear the questions he wants to spit at me. This was going to be a big project, and he would have made a lot of money on it.

I swallow hard, and my hand drops to my side. "I'm going back to my country, and I'm not sure when or if I'll be coming back."

He blows out a long, slow breath. "I see."

His curiosity is palpable. But I'm not in the business of sharing things so private. "I'm not sure what the process will entail, but I need to shift the money I have in that account to someone else."

"Someone else?"

I sigh. "Yeah. You grew up here, right? You know who I may have to talk to. I need to liquidate it and get it to Scarlett. Whether she likes it or not, she needs it for her rink." I'm not sure how aware Ash is regarding Scarlett's financial issues, and I'm not going to spread anything that she may not want me to share. All he needs to know is that the money needs to go to her. "Will you make sure she gets it? Before the new year?"

"I—sure—of course." So many questions in those few words. He pauses for a moment, then his voice comes through the receiver again. "It might take a few days to get it released. There will be paperwork, and there might be some fees."

"It's fine. See what you can do. I need her to have that money."

"Can I ask you why you don't just give it to her yourself?"

I consider telling him to mind his own business, but we've gotten closer over the last week. I may even call him a friend. A sigh escapes my lips, and I drag a hand down my face before quietly saying, "I don't think she'll accept it from me. She's always been more than a little stubborn. Since I'll be out of town, she won't have the option of throwing it back in my face."

All I hear is a soft chuckle from the man. Thank goodness he seems to understand.

"Thanks, Ash. I owe you."

"Just make sure if you do end up coming back that I'm the one you call." He doesn't have to explain. I know what he means. If I build a place of my own, he's my guy.

"Of course."

The following morning, I sit beside a sleepy and somewhat disappointed Annabelle in a large private jet. Across the aisle, James is looking at his phone, scrolling through what looks like news articles. He managed to strong-arm me into leaving today after he made a stop at Stella's for me while I packed.

The little red box on my lap has the last of Eve's sugar plums, which I've decided I can't live without. It will be worth a trip out to Idaho next year, if only to get her to fix up more for me to take home.

I'm tempted to pry the lid off and sneak a few of them, but I refrain.

It's as if eating them will destroy the last piece I have of this place—the last piece I have of Scarlett.

The scenery out the window rushes by as the plane takes off. We'd pulled some strings to use a small municipal airport rather than taking the drive to the city. Once in the air, I look over the top of Annabelle's head, and my eyes soak in the now-familiar Christmas town that stole my heart before I knew that was a possibility.

"We'll come back, right?" Annabelle whispers, turning her eyes up to me. "We'll visit Miss Scarlett and Meredith and Miss Holly?"

I pull her head into my chest before brushing a kiss to the top of her head. "I don't know, bug. But I hope so."

Chapter 21

SCARLETT

He's gone.

Kasper Montgomery is officially gone.

I can't believe I let it happen.

"It's not your fault," Holly says quietly over the top of her coffee mug.

My head whips up to stare at her, my eyes sharp. "Of course it's my fault. I didn't tell him to stay."

"You said that there was a family emergency."

"There is... but I didn't tell him I wanted him to stay with me. Or to come back or to..." My voice trails off. That's not the worst of this particular situation. I avoided him like the plague. I refused to talk to him after that last lesson with Annabelle. I'd thought I had more time. I'd thought after I let the idea of him leaving sink in, I would get the courage to tell him how I feel.

"You love him, don't you?"

I drop my eyes to my cup. It's untouched. I can't bring myself to drink from it.

I've lost him, and I won't be getting him back. That's been made very clear to me. He left without saying goodbye.

That's not entirely true. He sent several messages to me. He called me, too. He wanted me to meet up with him, and I didn't bother answering him.

Then Holly dropped the bomb that he'd left.

No amount of hot coffee will warm my soul now. I can't explain any of this. I'm a reasonable, levelheaded woman, and all I can think about is what I lost. "Yeah," I rasp. "I love him."

"Then you can't let him go."

She doesn't understand. I haven't told her what his family emergency entails. It's not my place. I can't tell her that Kasper is next in line to become king. She'd probably throw me a parade and call me the future queen of whatever that country is.

"I can't." It's all I can muster. What kind of person would I be if I called him and told him how much I missed him? It would only hurt both of us. I know it, and so does he. It's probably why he hasn't bothered calling or messaging me after I refused to talk to him.

Placing my elbows on the table, I push my head into my hands and let my fingers tangle in my hair. I used to be on top of the world. I had everything. I was happy.

And now look at me.

"So this is what rock bottom feels like."

"It's not over until it's over."

I snort a laugh. "I'm pretty sure this is over."

"I mean with the rink."

Slowly, I lift my head.

She's smiling at me, though the look is laced with pity. It's too hard for her to hide that she feels bad for me. Heck, I feel bad for me. I can't blame her one bit. She shifts in her seat and tilts her head as she taps her fingers on her mug. "You still have another week you can try to raise money."

"Holly," I groan, retuning my head to my hands. "We tried that. All month long I tried. And I still didn't make enough. What makes you think I can make up the difference by the end of the week? We have to face facts. I failed."

"You haven't failed yet," she insists. "What if we approach this project of yours from a different angle?"

"Yeah?" I mutter. "And how would you suggest I do that?" I don't have the energy to lift my gaze to meet hers. I don't have the energy for anything. Maybe I'll stay here at this table and let the world keep turning without me.

I feel her soft touch before I hear her words. "Maybe you need to be more upfront about what's going on. I've seen this town come together for their own. It happens all the time."

Probably shouldn't be rolling my eyes right about now. My friend confirms my suspicions when she scowls at me.

"I mean it."

"I'm not *people*," I remind her. "I'm a stranger."

She scoffs. "You're as much part of this town as I am, and I'm a transplant. People love you like they love Lucian, too. You're part of this place. I bet you anything if they knew you weren't going to be around anymore, they'd all step up to help."

I hate—no, despise—charity. At least for myself. I don't want people to know what happened to me. I just want to go about doing what I love.

Apparently, fate has something different in mind for me.

"What do you say? Can we do things my way this time? Let's throw one more party. I met a sweet girl in town the other day. She's a reporter."

I stiffen immediately, and Holly laughs.

"Don't worry. We can keep Kasper and all the craziness out of your story. We can get her to write a heartrending story about you and the rink—about you wanting to keep it going. If we get interest from people in the neighboring towns... who knows? It can't hurt, can it?"

I shrug. "I guess we haven't tried it yet."

"Darn straight, we haven't." She sits there in silence for a few minutes, and for the briefest of moments, I start to have a little bit of hope.

It's dangerous, that hope. It has the potential of tearing me apart if I'm not careful.

"So?"

I glance over to Holly. That wide, knowing smile is plastered all over her face.

"What?"

She wags her brows at me, and I groan.

"*What?*" I demand, sharper this time.

"We need to figure out a plan for you and Kasper."

I groan again, this time so loud that the table beside us shoots me a concerned look.

"What?" she laughs again. "You love him."

"So?"

"So..." she drawls. "He loves you, too."

"You don't know that."

"*Honey.*" Her voice drips with a plethora of emotions I can't decipher. "If that man doesn't love you, then up is down and black is white."

This time, I fight my eye roll. She's still so much in love with Lucian. They've been together for only a short time, but I can see they're the type of couple that will last until the end of the world.

But Kasper and me?

It was literally a fairytale.

"I'm not cut out for fairytales," I point out. "Nothing ever works out for me."

"You need to stop saying that stuff."

"Why not? It's true."

"Because we're the only masters of our futures. You said you love him. So do something about it."

"Yeah," I snort. "Like I can just commandeer a plane and fly out to the middle of wherever it is. Can you imagine the looks on his family's faces if I were to show up proclaiming my love for a guy who's supposed to be king one day?"

Her eyes go round like saucers, and that's when I know I made a mistake.

I clap a hand around my mouth and shake my head. "I mean *if* he ends up being king one day."

Her brows pull forward, and she leans in close. "Is that the emergency? Is something happening with the line of succession?"

I flush hot and bright, so much so I can see it on my nose. Shutting my eyes, I shake my head. "I can't talk about this."

"Scarlett! You have to tell me. I thought it was weird he didn't say goodbye when he left. He clearly cares for you. But if there are certain... expectations... then everything make sense."

"Yes, okay?" I hiss, leaning toward her. "There's a chance he's going to have to take his brother's place as next in line for the throne. He couldn't exactly stay here with that responsibility hanging over his head, now could he?"

She settles back on her seat, her lips forming a perfect little "o."

My shoulders slump. So much for keeping secrets. I know Holly won't say anything, and now that she knows, I can't say I won't miss her pushing me to chase after the guy.

Everything seems so finite now.

Kasper has gone home to fulfill duties I can't have anything to do with. He's going to make a great ruler one day, and I'm going to be here... hopefully still skating.

"I'm so sorry, Scarlett."

I huff, not daring to look at her. If I do, I know I'll cry. "It doesn't matter anymore. He's gone. There's nothing I can do about it. There's no way to change any of it."

Holly's quiet again. I only hear a faint sipping sound every so often. Then she places her cup on the table with a soft thud. "You know... just because he's gone and he might be king one day... doesn't mean..."

"Don't even say it," I mutter. This time I meet her gaze. "I'm not even going to entertain what you're going to say. I can't do anything about my relationship with Kasper. It's one of those things that I have to remember fondly and let go."

"But what if when everything settles down..." She purses her lips together, and her eyes practically beg me to consider what she's about to say. "You should visit him."

Nothing in this life would make me happier. But I can't say that to her. I can't tell her that if I could go back, I would do things differently. I would have told him I loved him. I would have told him I want to spend my life with him in whatever capacity I can—even if that means following him to a foreign country.

I can't tell her any of that.

Instead, I shrug my shoulders and murmur, "Yeah, maybe."

It's a half-hearted response at best, but it seems to be exactly what Holly wants from me.

After coffee, we head over to the rink to put together our plan. She calls Ivy, and I sit down in a last-minute interview for an article that will be put in tomorrow's paper.

We spend hours calling businesses and putting together new flyers.

I don't know how I feel about everyone knowing I'm going to lose the rink, even if they come out in droves to support me.

I guess that's what happens when the numbness takes over.

Because that's exactly how I feel.

I'm one hundred percent numb. While I'm willing to put forth one last effort in saving my rink, I'm utterly exhausted. Part of me looks forward to the new year because then I won't have to worry about any of this anymore. The deadline will have passed, and I can start fresh in the new year.

I may not ever appreciate Christmas the same way I used to. In fact, I'm sure I'll hate this holiday for years to come. I will forever associate Christmas with loss.

It's okay. That's what I keep telling myself. I learned so many valuable lessons this month.

As I climb into bed and stare at the dark ceiling overhead, I mutter those words aloud. "It's okay." A tear slips out of the corner of my eye and trickles into my hair. "It will be okay."

Rolling to my side, I place my hands beneath my cheek and close my eyes.

As cliché as the phrase is, I wholeheartedly admit that it's better to love Kasper and lose him than to have never experienced what it was like to be loved by him. I'll never regret the whirlwind romance I had with him.

Chapter 22

KASPER

Alex looks worse than I expected. He's frail, his are cheeks sallow—even his eyes are dull and lifeless. He's resting, surrounded by pillows and comforters that make him look smaller than he is. Light filters through the drapes of the enormous windows to the right, giving him an almost angelic glow if he didn't look so sick.

It feels cold in this room, even to me.

The second I stepped into the room, my eyes landed on him. I'm scared to move closer. It's like when I reach him, he'll give up living. James alluded to as much.

A lump forms in my throat. Thankfully, my mother took Annabelle to her room to unpack. I don't want her to see her uncle this way. Heck, I'm not sure I can handle what I'm seeing. There's a chair beside the bed, likely used by people in my family. Since my father is still in good health, he's not worried about the line of succession. It just means I need to start taking on the duties my brother can no longer handle.

Sitting on the edge of the chair, I watch my brother's chest rise and fall. It's somewhat labored, and once again, I'm terrified of being in here. What if he takes a turn for the worse? Can I handle that?

I reach toward him and take his hand in mine. He murmurs something and glances in my direction. A faint smile touching his lips. "Kas? Is that you?" he rasps.

My hand tightens on his. "It's me, Alex."

He sucks in a breath and shifts where he lays. "I knew you would come."

Guilt rips me to shreds. Had I known this was what was happening, I would have been here sooner. I bite back the words. They won't do either of us any good. I wish I knew why our parents didn't just tell me when it started. He was fine when I left at the beginning of December.

Alex gives me a wry smile. "James has been keeping me up to date on you. Sounds like you might have fallen for a girl?"

I wince. It's not a good enough reason not to be here for my brother.

He chuckles, but it's quieter than his usual boisterous laugh. "You gonna go back?"

"No use. Things have changed."

For a moment, I think Alex is going to argue with me, but he doesn't. The door opens to his room, and my mother pokes her head into the room. "Kasper? You're needed for that meeting with your father."

Alex must be able to see how *not* thrilled I am to have to go because he chuckles again. "Maybe I should be worried about you more than you should be about me."

I get to my feet and give Alex's hand one more squeeze. "I'll be back to visit you later."

He nods.

My mother's concerned gaze drifts to Alex before landing on me again. She looks worse for wear as well. They're all struggling with losing Alex. There's no telling how much longer he has.

I touch my mother's shoulder as I pass her. Neither of my parents are nearly as upset as I am about how long it took for me to come home. They're just glad I'm here. Doesn't matter how much I'm beating myself up, we're together again. A complete family for the last time.

Clouded and foggy. That's how the next few days feel. Every mundane meeting, every appointment that requires my attendance drags on endlessly. Every so often, James is included in these meetings, and I can tell he enjoys them more than I do. When I'm not in meetings, I'm spending time with Annabelle or Alex.

It's hard not to hate myself for my lack of interest in ruling. A man in my position shouldn't be going through the motions. I should want this, right?

"Do you have any sixes?" Annabelle asks Alex.

He shakes his head.

Today, he's looking a little more like himself. There's more color in his cheeks, but it comes and goes.

Alex smirks at his only niece. "Go fish."

She sighs and leans over, flashing her cards to everyone seated on Alex's bed when she reaches for a card.

I bite back a smile. These will be the memories she holds onto.

"I didn't know you knew about this game." Alex shifts in his seat to get comfortable, his question directed at Annabelle.

"I just learned it," she murmured. "Holly taught me."

Alex's eyes dart to meet mine, and he grins. "Is that who you spent most of your time with? Holly?"

She shakes her head. "Holly babysat me a few times when Daddy helped Miss Scarlett."

I hadn't talked much about anyone from Idaho with Alex. Maybe it's the guilt that keeps me quiet. Or maybe it's the pain that accompanies those memories. I don't need to linger on what I'll never have.

Alex levels me with a curious stare. "Who's Miss Scarlett?" He's asking Annabelle the question, but his eyes remain locked with mine.

Annabelle perks right up. "She's the best ice-skater. She taught me how to go fast and not fall down. She taught Daddy, too. And we got to go skating together and to the Christmas festival." She continues to ramble on even as I can see understanding fill Alex's expression. He knows what Miss Scarlett is to us. He knows she's the woman I left behind.

Shoot.

My brother tilts his head slightly, face full of amusement and perhaps a degree of pity.

I don't want pity. I don't need it.

"I'm fine," I mutter, even though he hasn't said anything.

Annabelle glances at me with curiosity. Confusion is there, too, and I force myself to smile at her. She's fully aware of how much I care for Scarlett. She'd been included in the plans for the house, for heaven's sake. I'm just lucky she hasn't said anything to anyone here.

A few more minutes pass, and a couple more cards are drawn from the pile.

"We're going to have a house there, you know."

I make a face. Dang it all! She isn't supposed to say any of that. I told her the chances of us going back were slim.

"You are, are you?" Alex smirks again. "What kind of house?"

Annabelle shrugs. "Ash says it's gonna be big enough for a whole family, so maybe you can visit."

And just like that, the temperature in the room cools significantly. Both Alex and I know he will never be able to visit Idaho. He'll be lucky to see the new year.

I chance a look in his direction and find him watching me, contemplating the meaning of Annabelle's confession. I'm not about to correct Annabelle in front of Alex. She doesn't need to hurt more than she already does.

"Annabelle, sweetie, will you go ask Nana to bring me some tea? My throat is a little dry." I'm not ready for her to hear we may never be going back. Alex needs to know I plan to do the right thing.

She nods, placing her cards face up before climbing off the bed and scurrying out of the room.

"So, there's a Miss Scarlett and a plan to build a house. I feel like I'm missing out on a great deal more information than you thought I should know." Alex places his own cards down and leans back against his pillows. "Care to share?"

I shake my head. "It doesn't matter. That part of my life is over."

Alex snorts. "Nothing is over until it's over."

"Well, this is over." I frown, not capable of looking him in the eye. "I can't go back—not when I have to be here to run things when Dad passes."

He rolls his eyes. "Then ask her to come. You can't help who you fall in love with. And after Rose—"

I hold up a hand. "I'm going to stop you right there. She's not the type of person who would like being here. She loves her freedom. If I were to ask her to come, it'd be like asking her to lock herself up into a box where she can't breathe."

"Are you sure you're not describing how you feel right now?" Alex crosses his arms and watches me carefully.

He's probably right, but I don't want to admit it.

"No one wants you to stay if you're not happy."

I scoff. "Happiness is never part of the equation."

"You don't really believe that, do you?" Disbelief fills his voice, and a different kind of pain fills his eyes, one I've never seen before. "Kasper, happiness matters. It always matters. If you don't want to be here—if your heart is somewhere else, then you should go to where it is."

"It's not that easy." I push myself off the bed and charge across the room, suddenly feeling suffocated. "I can't have this conversation with you. It's different for me. You always wanted it. You were excited to be part of our legacy."

"And you aren't." It's not a question. Alex shifts in the bed, but he doesn't get out from under the covers. "If you're going to be miserable, then relinquish the crown."

"Don't be an idiot, Alex. You know as well as we do that's not how it works." James's voice comes from the doorway, and I glance toward him. Yep. There it is. The confirmation neither one of us needs. "Kasper has a duty, and he's going to uphold it."

"I'm not an idiot. If anything, you two are the idiots. Who says we have to do things the exact way our ancestors have? Would it be easy? Maybe not. But there are *three* of us, and we all know the best option isn't Kasper."

I stiffen and turn to face my oldest brother, not sure if I should be hurt or relieved.

James snorts. "And the right person is who, *you*? I hate to break it to you, but you're not going to kick this—"

I flinch. The words are wracked with pain and perhaps a little accusation. None of us saw this coming. None of us wanted this. I stare at James, noting something I hadn't seen before. He's scared. I can't fault him for lashing out. His brothers were his whole world, growing up. And he would be losing us both.

"Oh, I'm well aware." Alex's soft words break through the silence. He isn't mad, though there is a degree of sadness to his words. Apparently, he's the only one who's come to terms with his diagnosis and that breaks my heart more than I'm prepared to admit. "*No*," Alex sighs, "I'm not talking about me—*clearly*. Kasper doesn't belong here. And you?" He stares James down. "You do."

This time James grows still.

"Wouldn't you like to be considered? We've all seen how well you do with parliament. We can tell you'd do a good job taking Dad's place. And Kas? He'd be free to have the life he dreams of with that ice-skater."

For a second, the room is deathly silent. I'm not even sure anyone is breathing. Alex looks between me and James as if daring either of us to argue. He's not dead yet, and as of this moment, he's got more sway with our parents when it comes to who should lead next.

He's right about one thing. Tradition states that I'm the next in line. But it's not unheard of for someone in my position to step down and give the opportunity to James, as long as we have the support of our family and the majority of the parliament.

I swallow hard and turn my searching gaze to James. I can tell he wants to take it—he just doesn't want to take it from me. For all intents and purposes, James is the only one standing in the way.

Alex is the first to break the silence with a laugh. "Look at you two. Sheesh, you'd think that the sky is going to crash around us if we do something slightly different than those in our past. Think about it. Take the night, if you have to. And when you decide, we can have a meeting with our parents and give them the good news."

James glances at me, then nods before he slips out of the room. A few moments later, Annabelle returns with a small tray and a steaming teacup. There are bits of the liquid on the tray surrounding the cup. Apparently, she needs a bit more practice at not letting the drink slosh while she walks.

Alex brightens at the sight of her. "There's my favorite girl."

She beams right back, a hint of the happiness returning to her gaze that I saw back in Idaho.

Maybe Alex is right.

Chapter 23

SCARLETT

"This is crazy!" Holly hurries toward me, her steps clunky with the skates on her feet. "Did you ever think there would be such a turn out?"

Ivy grins at my side, her hip propped against the counter. "I'm telling you, people are suckers for a good human interest story. I would know. I have to write so many." She releases an exaggerated groan.

Eying her, I'm tempted to ask her a few questions about her profession. For someone so good at their job, I'd think she'd love it more. She notices my stare and waves a dismissive hand before picking up her notebook.

Got it. She doesn't want to talk about it right now.

Turning, I take in the amount of people swarming my rink. I don't recognize several faces, which means Ivy's article reached a demographic I wasn't expecting. I've almost made more money tonight than I did during the last couple of skate nights combined.

Holly said it best. This is definitely crazy.

I should be thrilled.

Heck, I should be jumping up and down, squealing with delight alongside my friend.

But something is missing.

Two somethings, if I'm honest.

I haven't heard from Kasper since he left almost a week ago. I don't know why I expected him to call. He's going to be a king. Surely he's busy with more important things. Still, the ache in my chest won't dissipate as I dwell on the fact that he should be here.

Ivy nudges me. "You okay?" She says it quietly enough that Holly can't hear me from where she's watching the event play out.

I nod, not meeting her gaze.

It's another strange sort of occurrence—befriending Ivy. She grew up in Breckenridge, but she lives in McCall. She writes for the paper that serves most of the surrounding cities. If I had to guess, I'd think she wishes she could move on to something grander. Ivy's the kind of girl who dreams big.

She's a spitfire, too—something I need when it comes to saving this place. She tells it how it is, and she doesn't shy away from anything.

Ivy's green eyes narrow at me, and she tilts her head. There's that determination I still haven't gotten used to. Before she's able to pester me further, Holly spins to face us, her hands on the counter. "Lucian says he's going to stop by."

Ivy perks up, her reporter ears practically burning.

Holly rolls her eyes. "You already wrote a piece about him moving to town. I've seen it."

Our friend pouts. "But those articles get me noticed more."

Her eyes sweep over Holly's slight form, and she taps her chin with a finger. "Are you sure you two aren't expecting? Nothing will hit better than gossip that's actually true—"

Holly snorts. "No. And even if I was, I wouldn't be doing a tell-all to the paper." Her eyes drift to mine, and her mouth twitches.

My lips part. She's totally pregnant. My best friend is going to be a mom. Now I feel like I should be jumping up and down with her. I don't. Pressing my lips into a thin line, if only to keep myself from smiling or saying something stupid, I return my focus to the spreadsheet on my laptop.

"How's it going so far?" Holly leans over the counter as if she'll be able to make sense of what's on my screen.

"We're doing really well. But we haven't had a new customer in over an hour. I don't think I'll be making much more tonight. It's getting late." I chew on my thumb. I'll be a couple thousand short. There's a small chance that I can get an extension—but it's slim. I really don't want to risk it.

"How much do you need?"

Distractedly, I lift my gaze to Holly, then do a double take and shake my head. "No. I'm not going to let you cover the difference. How many times do we have to go through this?"

"Come on, Scarlett! You can't keep doing this. At some point, you have to accept that your friends are here to help, even if you don't want it."

The problem isn't that I don't want it. The problem is how much I do. But if I allow myself to lean on them this time, what will happen if I falter again? I can't keep asking for support. "I have to do this on my own." A groan spills from my lips. "Things weren't great when I was a kid. I had to depend on others just to survive."

"All kids—" Holly starts, but I interrupt her.

"All kids could trust their caregivers. I couldn't." The pain threatens to swallow me whole. "I had to depend on the kindness of strangers, teachers, social workers." It's not a story I've told entirely and I don't dare to look my friends in the eye. "When I left that life, I swore it would never happen again." I rub at my heart on my chest. "As stupid as it might sound, I need to count on me." They're quiet for a moment, then Holly speaks again.

"But you would have let Kasper help you," she points out.

I feel two sets of eyes drilling into me after those words fill the void between us. Ivy and Holly have teamed up against me more than once. They're at it again. The worst part is that they're wearing me down. I don't know how much longer I can fend them off before I finally succumb to the pressure.

"She's right, you know," Ivy murmurs. "If you were going to let Kasper—"

"I was only going to let Kasper help when I thought he was moving here and we were going to..." My voice catches in my throat. When we were going to... *what*? There hadn't been a proposal. And now he's gone. I shake my head again, hating the blush that threatens to overtake my whole body. "None of that matters. He's gone. I'm doing this on my own. And if you two are my friends, then you're going to let me do things my way."

I don't miss the way they share a look. After tonight, I'll know where I stand. And then we won't have this conversation anymore.

The rest of the evening is more of the same. I lose track of how many times I calculate and count the money. My head hurts, and my muscles ache from being so tense.

Holly spends an hour with her husband skating while they hold hands. Ivy sighs, leaning on the counter with one elbow, her hand propping her head up.

I glance at her with amusement. "No one special, huh?"

She shakes her head. "I'm too busy."

Arching a brow, I smirk at her. "You're here, though."

"Yeah," she drawls, "because I want to support you. And I want to see if my article did anything."

I scoff, gesturing wildly at the throngs of people still filling the rink. "I think it's safe to say you made a difference."

She shrugs, her eyes following other couples as they make the rounds. *I'll be Home for Christmas* plays over the loudspeaker. I know how she feels. There's something about being alone at Christmastime that sits different.

"Maybe you should make more time for it."

"For what?" she muses.

"A relationship."

Ivy snorts. "Even if I made time, this area isn't exactly flooded with eligible bachelors. Most of the guys here are taken or... weird."

"What about Ash?" I don't know the guy well, but Kasper seems to like him.

There's a brief moment when Ivy's whole body goes rigid. Then she turns her head toward me and wrinkles her nose. "Have you met Ash?"

I snicker. "Clearly. I wouldn't have suggested him if I hadn't."

She huffs, standing upright. "He's my brother's best friend and he's... terrible."

"Really? He seems pretty nice to me."

Ivy groans. "Sure. He's nice to the people he cares about."

I turn to face her and fold my arms, my curiosity piqued. "But not to you?"

The look she launches at me says it's best not to know. And now that's the only thing I want.

"What happened?"

She huffs. "Let's just say that he's always been that spoiled rich kid, and I'm not worth the mud under his boots."

I didn't get that feeling at all when I met the man. He's smart and accommodating. If what she says about his wealth is true, then he's very down to earth.

Ivy wags a finger in my face. "I haven't known you long, but I know that look. Don't get any ideas. He's not going to be anyone's knight in shining armor. You'd be better off steering clear of him."

Does she think that I'm interested in the guy?

Nothing can be further from the truth. I'm still nursing my wounded heart that Kasper abandoned here on the ice.

Her eyes shift toward the door, and once again, she freezes. "I knew I shouldn't have talked about him. He's like Beetlejuice. You say his name three times and he appears." Her lips curl with disgust, and I whip my head around to find Ash striding toward us.

My eyes bounce from Ash to Ivy and back. The former slows his gait when he notices Ivy. I half-expect him to stop where he stands or turn around and head out of here like his clothes have caught fire. But he doesn't.

Ash rolls his shoulders and straightens a bit before returning his gait to a brisk walk. He doesn't deign a look in Ivy's direction when he stops at the desk where we stand.

The usual easy smile I'm used to isn't anywhere to be seen. In its place is a strained one that makes me want to give him a little shake. Ash's hazel-brown eyes flick around the rink at the turn out. "Looks like you've made something here."

Ivy snorts, earning a sharp look from Ash. It's so quick that I don't think Ivy notices. Then again, maybe she does, because in the very next second she storms off.

Ash relaxes visibly, his eyes following her for a moment. He glances toward me, and I swear I can see a flush creep into his ears. "How are you doing, Scarlett?"

I lift my brows. His question knocks me off balance. I don't know him well enough for him to be worried about me. Ignoring the question, I gesture to the wall of skates. "Would you like to rent some skates tonight?"

He shakes his head, and I try not to feel disappointed. Every little bit helps. Ash takes me in. His eyes are more discerning than I had given him credit for. "Really, how are you? Have you heard from Kasper?"

Heat floods my body—but not the enjoyable kind. Embarrassment and pain hit me like the frigid, ice-cold air when it dips below freezing. Pressing my lips into a thin line, I shake my head.

Ash frowns, then reaches into his breast coat pocket and retrieves an envelope. Had Kasper written me a letter?

I eye the white envelope like it's going to bite me if I'm not careful. Never have I wanted something so badly while being terrified to have it at the same time. When I look back to Ash, he's watching me with curiosity. "What is that?" I ask.

"Kasper—"

"Don't tell me he wrote me a break-up letter. It's pretty clear where he stood when he took off without saying goodbye."

Ash goes still, his fingertips resting on the envelope that he's placed between us on the counter. "He didn't say goodbye?"

I flush angrily. "I really don't want to talk about this. You might as well take that letter and give it right back to him."

He pushes the envelope closer to me. "It's not a letter."

"Regardless, I don't want it."

"I think you should open it." His voice is calm, gentle—so at odds with the strong, angular man who stands before me.

I consider snatching it and tearing it in two, but I know the second I touch it, I'll open it to see what he said.

Ash nudges it again, then steps back. "He wanted you to have this. After everything that's happened, he insisted." He nods at me, then strides away without another word.

"What did he want?" Ivy snaps, her voice dragging me from my stupor.

I turn my eyes to the envelope. "Kasper wants me to have that."

"What is it?" Ivy reaches for the envelope without permission and tears it open. Then she pulls out a single slip of paper, and her eyes double in size. She flips it around to show me. "Look at all those zeros."

Chapter 24

KASPER

I should have come sooner.

Alex had insisted I do as much, but the guilt had been backbreaking. As of yesterday, he was feeling better. The doctor said this happens. Alex was still dying. All we could do was enjoy the time we had.

But my stubborn brother practically threw me on the plane and told me to win her back, all the while swearing he didn't plan on crossing over to the other side before I came back.

I don't even know if she's going to want to see me. Beyond the simple thank you she sent in a text, I've heard nothing else. I should be grateful she didn't bite my head off when I gave her no choice but to accept the money.

What am I doing?

From the outside, the rink looks the same. It's still here. It's still standing.

I hate how much my chest aches from seeing the familiar structure. If Scarlett refuses to see me, I don't know what I'll do.

Three days.

That's all I have before I have to go back home.

Three days to try to win back the girl I fell in love with over the last four weeks.

The town is quiet. No one shuffling from storefront to storefront to go shopping. Stella's is closed, too. But of course it is. New Years Day is something that should be spent with family—or perhaps folks just haven't crawled out of bed yet after a night of celebrating.

Snow glitters on the sidewalks and streets. Few tire tracks have disturbed the magical feel of this small town. The sky is a brilliant blue today, allowing the sun to bounce off every ice crystal in the immediate vicinity.

I shove my hands into my pockets and contemplate what may happen next. If Scarlett turns me away, I fully intend on pestering her until she agrees to speak to me. The whole flight here, I practiced my speech, and it still doesn't feel like enough.

Ash, the scoundrel, didn't stick around to see Scarlett's reaction to the check he delivered. Instead, he told me I deserved the discomfort of wondering. In his words, "Who leaves the love of their life without saying goodbye?"

Apparently, I do.

My sigh sends a white puff into the air, and it dissipates before my eyes.

You came all this way.

What are you waiting for?

Just go in there and tell her you can't live without her.

I duck my head. There's no way I'll go home now that I'm here. I may as well get it over with. I haven't bothered calling her. What would I say? Then again, she might have hung up on me, and I wasn't prepared for that. The door to the rink may very well be locked, and I may not be able to avoid having a phone conversation with her anyway.

So many thoughts spin in my mind until I reach the front door and pull on the handle.

It gives way.

For a few minutes, I stand there, stunned the door opened at all. Is she open? Has she forgotten to lock it?

Shaking off the questions, I slip inside. It's dim, with the only light coming from the windows high up on the wall. The quiet is immediately sliced to smithereens when the speakers belt out an orchestra performance of "The Dance of the Sugar Plum Fairy." It's one of my favorite musical compositions from the ballet. Not for the first time, I'm frozen to my spot. There's no sign of Scarlett —not at the counter. Not on the ice.

I glance around where I stand in the entrance, wondering if I should head back to her office, when I see her.

Gone are the jeans, jacket, and gloves she normally wears on the ice.

Today, she's clad in a sparkling leotard and skirt. It gives the appearance of Scarlett being wrapped in glitter. The white fabric hugs her form, curving up over her chest in a swirl and around her lower back, showing off some skin. The sheer skirt ruffles as she picks up speed and leaps into the air.

I'm completely transfixed. Not a single muscle in my body can move from where I'm rooted. She glides and skates over the ice like she was born to it. And maybe she was. How did I forget that she competed against the best the world had to offer?

I shiver as she continues her performance, wanting nothing more than to skate out there and pull her into my arms. As if my legs decide on their own, I move toward the darkened reception counter.

With skates on my feet and my inhibitions buried so deep I know I'm in for a great deal of trouble, I move toward the ice.

The second metal meets the frosty surface, she skids to a stop. A gasp tears from her throat, and her wide eyes take me in.

"Kasper?" Her whisper reaches me just before she surges forward.

I only make it a quarter of the way toward her before she collides with me, knocking the two of us off our feet. I grunt, and pain rips through my backside, but all I see is her.

Scarlett's bright blue eyes find mine, and she searches my face. "It's really you," she breathes out. "You're really here."

Chuckling, I brush a strand of hair from her face. "I'm really here."

She throws her arms around me, clinging to me, and that's when I feel her body shudder.

"Are you—Scarlett, are you crying?"

The woman has the gall to shake her head, but she won't look at me.

"Hey," I murmur, attempting to pull her away so I can get a better look at her. "What's the matter?" When I successfully get a good look at her, I find tears sliding down her flushed cheeks. "Should I leave?"

Scarlett's eyes widen, and she shakes her head with a growl. "Don't you dare."

Her response has me laughing. "Then why are you so upset?" I place a hand to her cheek and brush at a tear with my thumb. "I've only been gone a couple days."

"Ten days," she mutters.

I laugh again. "Ten," I amend. Has it really been that long?

Scarlett pulls away from me, getting to her feet before offering me her hand. I'm not proud of how difficult it is to get to an upright position, but at this point, I don't care. The second I'm stable, I pull her in for another hug, and she clings to me like before.

All that worrying. All that fretting. It was for nothing.

"Thank you," she whispers.

I don't have to ask her what she's referring to. "You're welcome." I wait a moment, then murmur, "So they allowed you to keep it." It wasn't a question.

She rubs her face into my coat, then looks up at me. "Apparently someone called the bank and pulled some strings."

There's no use biting back the smile I wear. I'd always planned on being her failsafe. Even when I funded the project with Ash. Scarlett just hadn't been aware of it. I rub my thumb against her cheek again. "Sounds like you have a guardian angel looking after you."

"Sounds like." She watches me for a moment, then she looks around. "Where's Annabelle?"

"Home."

The frown that crosses her face threatens to tear my heart apart all over again. "You're not staying."

"I have to go back in three days."

Her hold on me tightens, and she sighs. "I knew it was too good to be true."

"What is?" I don't know if I want her answer. The question slipped from my lips before I realized it.

Scarlett shakes her head. "It doesn't matter."

I pull back and lift her chin with my finger and thumb. "I'm coming back," I assure her. The guarded confusion in her gaze spurs me onward. "I'm stepping down—giving the throne to James. I don't want to be king—never have."

"It doesn't work that way—" she blusters.

"You sound a lot like James when you say that."

She frowns, and I laugh. "It's not the norm, no. But it's an option. James will be an excellent heir, and I'm going to try to get dual citizenship here."

Scarlett gasps. I didn't think her eyes could grow any wider than a few minutes ago, but I'm wrong. "You're... staying? For good?"

I lean forward and kiss her nose. "If you'll have me."

Without warning, she reaches up and captures my face with both of her hands. Her kisses flutter from my lips to my jaw and along my throat before returning to my mouth. She's on her toes, giving me every part of her.

"Is that a yes?" I let out the second she gives me a chance to breathe.

"That's a yes," she whispers back.

I press my forehead to hers. "I want you to know I still plan on building that house. I want to have it started and ready for when Annabelle comes back here."

Her eyes swim with emotion. "I like that idea." Then her happy expression falters, and she pulls back suddenly. "The money you had set aside for the house—"

Holding a finger to her lips, I grin. "It was money well-spent. And there's more where that came from."

Scarlett's lips part. She blinks several times, then holds a hand to her chest. She closes her mouth, then opens it again.

I can't help the chuckle that rumbles through my chest. It feels good to laugh with her. A future with this woman is something I gave up on, and yet here we are. "I love you," I murmur.

The shock prevents her from speaking. Her face flushes, and tears return to her eyes. "You do?"

"Of course I do. I thought that was understood. I mean... why else would I upend my entire life to move to a place like this?"

She smirks. "I don't know... Stella's is pretty great."

I throw my head back and let out a mock groan. "You're right. Stella's makes the move so worth it."

"*Hey!*" Scarlett's laughing.

I turn serious eyes back to hers. "Stella's might be the sugar on top, but you? You're everything." I hook my finger beneath her chin and tilt it so there's no chance for her to look away. "I'm so in love with you, I'd move here just so I could have a chance to catch a glimpse of you every day. Nothing would make me happier than sharing my life with you—to take care of you, even though everyone knows you can take care of yourself."

She laughs, another tear slipping down her cheek. "I'd like that."

"Good. Because one day, Scarlett Winters, I'm going to make you mine."

Chapter 25

Six Months Later

SCARLETT

"Don't open your eyes."

I laugh. "If I did, I'm pretty sure you'd poke my eye out because your hands are glued to my eyes." I stumble forward as Kasper moves me through the house that's only just been framed. It's hot, and a gentle breeze whistles through the wooden beams.

"Good."

I snicker.

Kasper guides me carefully across wooden floorboards. Based on the twists and turns, I get the sense we're entering what would be the kitchen. While we're not officially engaged, Kasper made it clear in no uncertain terms that one day this house will belong to the both of us.

"What are you so excited about?" I can't keep the glee out of my voice. I love this side of Kasper. His enthusiasm for life continues to fuel me, making my existence something I will never take for granted.

A few weeks ago, we renovated the roof of the rink, adding enormous skylights so we can skate beneath the stars in the evening. That was a surprise, too. If this surprise is anything like that one, I'm going to love it.

Kasper pulls us to a stop. Anticipation sizzles between us. His voice lowers. "Before I show you, I need you to know that every single step of building this house, I've been thinking about you. I want you as happy as I am when I'm with you."

I place my hands on his wrists and croon. "I'm happy when I'm with you, too."

"Good." He slowly lowers his hands. It takes a few moments for my eyes to adjust to the sunlight of the afternoon. Blurry greens and browns focus into lush trees and the beginnings of a beautiful landscape.

Then I see it.

A large pond has been dug behind the house. We stand on the back porch, and I can already imagine what the view will look like after the first snow fall. It's definitely man-made, but care has been taken to ensure it matches the scenery around us.

I gasp and whirl to find Kasper kneeling behind me. In his hand he holds a beautiful diamond ring. His eyes are bright, full of love only for me.

"Scarlett, I—"

Flinging my arms around his neck, I throw myself into him, knocking us both off balance. He catches himself so we don't completely crash onto the floor. "Yes!" The word bursts from somewhere deep inside my chest. "Yes, I'll marry you."

He places his hands on either side of my face and kisses me deeply. The electricity of his touch ripples through my body, from where our mouths meet right down to my toes. This man can make me forget all my worries while replacing them with hope. He knows me better than I know myself.

After our kiss, our foreheads touch. The only sound I can hear is the evidence of our breathless kiss. My heart hammers, and my pulse thrums, happily singing and dancing to music only it can hear. "I love you," I whisper. "So much."

"I love you, too."

I lift my hand and stare at the ring. "So... when should we do the honors?"

He smirks, and I laugh.

"What?"

Kasper takes my hand in his before he runs this thumb over my knuckles. "When I marry you, we'll be surrounded by snow." He gestures around us. "Maybe we'll even do it here."

I curl into him, admiring the ring on my finger. "I think that sounds absolutely perfect."

December 1st

SNOW FALLS OUTSIDE THE FLOOR-TO-CEILING WINDOWS of my large kitchen. The flakes practically glow beneath the light of the full moon and the porch lights I turned on so I can watch the first winter storm of December.

The hum of voices float through my future home. The turnout for the housewarming party is over the top. With over five thousand square feet, we have the room to spare, and yet it feels almost a little overcrowded.

I lean against the counter in the kitchen, my hands wrapped around a steaming mug of hot chocolate as the doorbell rings. Annabelle darts from the back door and charges toward the entrance, likely to see who her father will welcome inside.

In moments like this one, it's hard to remember what life was like before Kasper and Annabelle entered my life. Those memories feel like a lifetime ago. My life truly feels like a fairytale.

Eva sweeps into the kitchen with her husband Nick on her heels. She sets down a large red pastry box with a flourish.

"Eva! You didn't," I gush, moving closer.

"Of course I did. And I always will."

"Don't tell me you brought more of those delicious sugar plums." Kasper's voice arrives before he materializes. In seconds, he's standing behind me, his arms circling my waist. I lean into him, taking in his spiced scent.

Eva rolled her eyes. "I never showcase the same thing two years in a row. You should know that about me. Always onward and upward to better things."

I can practically feel the smirk that crosses my fiancé's lips. "Oh? And what will you be spotlighting this year?" Kasper leans forward to take a look into the box as Eva carefully takes the lid off.

Her show draws the attention of several others in the immediate vicinity. Holly and Lucian come closer with Ivy in tow. On the other side of the room Meredith glances up from where she's speaking to Ash.

Eva reaches into the box and pulls out a small tart with red filling. "Cranberries."

My stomach gurgles, eliciting a chuckle from Kasper. Holly adjusts her hold on her new baby, swaying back and forth. She's the one who speaks first when Ivy reaches into the box to grab one of the tarts. "Be careful, Ivy. I wouldn't be so enthused about eating one of Eva's desserts unless you're ready to fall in love."

Ivy's hand pauses above the box. Those standing around the counter go quiet before the mayor lets out a deep chuckle.

"Don't believe a single thing she tells you. My wife may be one of the best pastry chefs this side of the country, but she's not magic."

"No, but her sweets are," Holly insisted. "Scarlett, tell her. The desserts at Stella's are magic."

I roll my eyes with a laugh. "I think it's all pure coincidence."

"Coincidence? You found yourself a literal prince. Poof! Out of nowhere, and you're in love."

Kasper's arms tighten on me, and I crane my head around to look at him. "Sure, let's call it magic. Magic of the Christmas season. Magic of delectable desserts. Or just plain magic of true love's kiss."

A couple more chuckles make the rounds in our group. Eva offers the tart in her hands to Ivy. "You know the legend, right? The magic well that used to be in the center of this town? Nick thinks Stella's sits on that well. It's all just stories, but it's fun to believe in something like true love, right?"

I don't miss the way Ivy's gaze darts across the room to where Ash still speaks to Meredith. He doesn't glance in her direction. In fact, they've been careful not to bump into each other all evening.

Ivy offers Eva a tentative smile. "I'm a journalist. I don't believe in true love—not in the traditional sense."

"That's a pity." Eva tilts her head, her eyes sparkling with delight. "Life would be utterly boring without it."

❄ ❄ ❄

COME TO BRECKENRIDGE AND STAY AWHILE. THERE'S going to be plenty of excitement at the Frosted Wonderland.

Ivy wants out of Idaho, and the fastest ticket is through a promotion. But she's going to have to get along with the one man who can't seem to stand her in order to get it. Will she survive this final writing assignment? Find out in A Cranberry Wish.

About the Author

Kari Shuey is a resident of Idaho with her family of six. She's a master creator so you can almost always find her drawing, baking, sewing, or writing. Clean romantic suspense and sweet contemporary romance are her favorite genres. If you like emotional tension, the perfectly placed red herring, or sweet happily ever afters, then you'll love her other works. Don't miss out on her bi-monthly newsletters for fun updates on her books, crazy life, recommended reading, and more.

Sign up for my newsletter here: https://sendfox.com/lp/m2yz55